DREAM WALKER

BY CRYSTAL INMAN

All Rights Reserved

"Cowards die many times before their deaths; the valiant never taste of death but once."
Julius Caesar, Act 2, Scene 2

William Shakespeare

CHAPTER 1

Rissa killed six men at the age of six and became the world's youngest serial killer. She simply thought she destroyed her most-hated toy. The brutal truth being, she slaughtered half a dozen diplomats in four different countries. It was a home run for her handlers, and the beginning of a booming career for the young girl.

There would be no DNA. No pesky evidence. Rissa could dream walk. Enter another person's dream as easy as walking through a doorway into another room. Not only could she enter dreams, she influenced them. Changed them. Altered them, if you will, in the real world.

Whatever Rissa wanted to happen, happened. She held the power of the dream. A raw talent to shape a life while in another's mind. They found and twisted her to their whims.

It wasn't as simple as ABC, no, not quite. The handlers instructed the retrievers to start small. Chat up the nearby homeless. Give them food and drink. Appear non-threatening. Ingratiate themselves. Then bring a piece of them back to the lab.

That's how it started. Rissa didn't hate anything, but there were things she hated. A puppet show with a mean character. Shouts. Mistreated animals. Her handlers learned all her buttons.

They planted the seed by showing Rissa the "mean" homeless person, and then they placed the related piece of clothing in her bed that evening. Her subconscious finished the process. Bodies piled up. They praised her the next day and offered an extra dessert.

A child serial killer trained by using her natural sympathy and love of desserts as leverage.

The real test came, and the Retrievers collected pieces of clothing across the globe. All of their work handed over to a mere child. The handlers warned they best have the right trigger.

The doctors asked what toy she didn't like, and Rissa didn't even have to think hard. She had a jack-in-the-box when she was younger, and she hated it. The handle on the side turned to make the scratchy music that hurt your ears. The scary pictures on the sides of the box. Then the music stopped, and the lid sprang open. A painted person popped up, and it gave her nightmares. Daddy thought it was funny. Mama threw it away.

The doctors explained it was an important night, and Rissa would have to sleep in a hospital bed for them to make sure she was safe, and they marched her into a big room with a large bed in the center.

Machines surrounded it, and Rissa balked. They bribed her with talk of a sucker afterwards, and she reluctantly let them lift her onto the bed.

One doctor put sticky things on her and told her he would monitor her heart and blood pressure. Rissa didn't like the things on her skin.

The handlers kept her up past her bedtime and finally put an overtired cranky little girl to bed with a hideous jack-in-the-box next to her pillow. The hated toy with pieces of clothing from incredibly important men from across the globe. Rissa pressed up as close to the side rails of the bed as she possibly could and squeezed her eyes tight.

Rissa fell asleep to the sound of the jack-in-the-box music echoing in her head and a frown etched on her face.

****

Rissa walked into the room with a table top of the hideous toys. Each toy had a different odd hat on, but all she could see were the twisted grins and grotesque faces. New scary things painted on the sides like snakes and spiders. Her doctors wanted her to destroy each box any way she wanted.

She twisted one Jack's head off and pulled another from his box. She found scissors and cut two up. Only a couple left. Rissa frowned and looked at the last two boxes. She hated this game. Other games were more fun. Sometimes, they would let her play dress-up. Rissa wore fancy shoes with shiny pieces on them. They always took them away when she finished. They never gave them back. Rissa rolled her eyes. She beat one Jack's head on the table until the plastic split right down the center. She studied the last one. It seemed to stare straight at her. She grabbed the scissors and stuck them right in Jack's eye.

Satisfied, Rissa scooted off the table and waited. They woke her, and she sat up. The main doctor handed her a cherry sucker with a small smile. Rissa told him she wanted the grape. She licked her cherry sucker and glared at the doctor. He left quickly and shut the door behind him. Maybe he was afraid he would be in one of her dreams, too.

Rissa rolled her eyes and sighed as a nurse escorted her back to her room. Tiny bare feet pattered on the cold tile as her small scrubs fluttered in the halls slight breeze. Bleach, the ever-present smell, made her tired eyes water.

The nurse opened her door, and Rissa stepped inside. She licked her sucker and glanced around. Her bedroom looked and felt like a hospital room. It was the first time she noticed.

This was supposed to be a school. Where were the other students? When were her parents going to come and visit? She plopped down on her bed and scowled out the window beside it. Her head hurt from the dream and lack of sleep.

The sun rose slowly and shone its first few rays into Rissa's room.

She held her tired face up to it and tried to remember this was only for a month or two. A couple of months at this school with bare walls and rude doctors. Then she could go home.

CHAPTER 2

Marcus and Elizabeth Clay married after a short six-month engagement. Elizabeth, much older at thirty-two, didn't see the point of waiting. Marcus, twenty-four and fresh out of college, would do anything to please his polished fiancée. Elizabeth came with her own home, job, and car. Marcus had one, would gain one when married, and was on a desperate search for the third.

They were a handsome couple. Marcus a couple inches taller than Elizabeth, unless she wore heels. His short blond hair a perfect foil for her long scarlet tresses. Their green eyes contrasted but complemented each other. Marcus with the dark green you swore looked like ocean depths. Elizabeth with the pale green that conjured thoughts of seafoam in the morning sun.

He looked aristocratic with sharp angles and thin lips but built as though he could catch or throw a football at any minute. A juxtaposition of appearances. Marcus never knew which side to play up.

She didn't have a care what people thought. Elizabeth could wear jeans or silk and still be both friendly and elegant. She'd saved Marcus many times when he wandered away from a conversation flummoxed by what he heard. Intelligent, sweet, and patient. Marcus could not have been luckier.

Elizabeth was his everything.

Their wedding was simple. Elizabeth had no family. They'd passed in an auto accident two summers previous. Marcus had a father who lived in the bottom of a whiskey bottle. They had friends stand for them and began their life together.

It wasn't a surprise when Elizabeth became pregnant almost immediately. Marcus still hadn't found a job, but they weren't hurting for money. Elizabeth would work up until her due date, and she had maternity leave. Marcus fixed the spare bedroom into a nursery with neutral colors of green, grey, and peach. Both wanted to be surprised.

Clarissa Elizabeth Clay arrived on a snowy February fourth in the wee hours of the morning. Her mother labored for nearly twelve hours, and her father stayed and supported her the entire time. She came out quietly, this girl, with red fuzz upon her head and light green eyes that seemed bigger than her face.

"Oh, Lizzie, she's beautiful," Marcus whispered. Tears slid down his cheeks and landed on his wife's shoulder.

Elizabeth cradled the newborn in her left arm and reached up with her right to wipe her husband's tears. "She is at that."

****

Clary Clay grew to be an active child who kept her parents on their toes.

"Is Clary in the kitchen?"

"I thought she was with you!"

"Oh, shit! Look outside!"

And there she would be. Sitting in the dirt. Face in the sunshine. Talking to the flowers or the neighborhood cat or the book she brought out.

Her parents admonished her every time, and Clary would simply study them with those big seafoam green eyes, and do it again.

Child gate. Locked door. Fence. It never mattered the barrier. Clary wanted out. Clary went out.

One night, when Clary was three, she escaped outside four times in a row.

Elizabeth and Marcus lay in bed, exhausted.

"Did you have sex with Houdini?" Marcus glanced over at Elizabeth.

Elizabeth laughed. "Yes, you ass." She shook her and sighed. "How in the hell is she doing it? It's like she knows."

Marcus groaned and fell back. "Beats me. Let's slap an ankle monitor on her."

"You fall asleep. I'll watch her." Elizabeth kissed her husband and shuffled into the living room. She had a good view of Clary's room and the back door. They put a bell high on the back door as the last two nights, their sweet escapist hadn't been satisfied with only her daily escapades. The moon seemed to want to play, also.

Elizabeth's mind wandered off, and she slumbered.

"Mama."

Elizabeth woke up to see Clary on her lap. Clary had her night clothes on and now her little cow slippers.

"Clary! You know you should be in bed! Your Daddy and I have told you."

"But, Mama! I am in bed."

Elizabeth frowned. "Now, Clary. You know better."

Clary sighed and slid off of her Mama's lap. She grabbed her hand and tugged her toward her bedroom.

Elizabeth let herself be taken, in fact, so she could prove to her daughter she needed to be in bed. She watched the back of her little redhead and smiled. Precocious and precious. They were blessed.

Clary led her through the doorway and pointed. "See?"

Elizabeth smiled and lifted her head, prepared to make her case, when the smile slid from her face. Clary was, indeed, in bed sleeping. Elizabeth looked down at the small hand she was holding.

"I'm dreaming," she muttered.

Clary smiled. "Me, too, Mama." She tugged her Mama's hand again. "Look at me." Then Clary let go. She hopped on the bed and took her own hand.

"Stop!" Elizabeth's voice came out thin as a reed.

"Why?" Clary frowned.

"You might hurt yourself."

"Oh." Clary carefully put her sleeping hand down.

"Is this how you go outside?"

Clary looked down.

"Clarissa Elizabeth Clay. Is this how you are going outside?"

"Yes, Mama." Clary raised her head. "I see where you and Daddy put the keys in your head, or how to unlock the lock when you're sleeping."

Elizabeth sat before she fell. She scooped Clary on her lap and held her tight. She kissed her daughter's hair and rocked her back and forth. What did they need to do to protect their child?

****

Marcus didn't buy Elizabeth's explanation at first. It took three dream visits from his daughter and wife to convince him. He didn't look at either the same.

"She can meander around in our heads when we're asleep, Liz. Jesus Christ." Marcus threw up his hands. "Doesn't that creep you out at all?"

"She's a child, Marcus! She's not in there scavenging for porn sites. Clary wanted a way to go outside."

"And when she wants a way to know what she's getting for her birthday? Or is mad when she doesn't receive what she wanted?

Am I not supposed to be worried about falling asleep that night?"

"We can work with her. She's a child. We are her parents. We are here to teach her. Guide her. Protect her."

"Protect her?" Marcus snorted. "Who's going to protect me?"

****

It all came to a head the first week of kindergarten. The principal called Marcus in to let him know about a fight between Clary and one of the other children, a little girl named Madison. Madison pushed Clary on the playground, and the teacher put Madison in a timeout.

The next day, as soon as Madison saw Clary, Madison screamed and cried that Clary hurt her. The teacher couldn't calm her down, and her mother needed to be called. Did Clary say anything about the fight to him?

"Not a word," he promised. But why would she need to, he thought. Marcus picked up Clary after school and drove home in silence. He parked the car and looked at his daughter.

"Did you hurt a little girl named Madison?"

Clary looked at him with those big light green eyes. "She hurt me first." Then she calmly hopped out of the car and walked into the house.

Marcus confronted Elizabeth when she came home, and she talked to Clary. Yes, Clary visited the little girl in a dream and pushed her. Yes, she was sorry. Yes. She promised she wouldn't do it again. Marcus didn't believe his daughter's promises. He started taking a prescription pill which prohibited dreaming.

They kept Clary in school another month until a little boy threw a toy truck at Clary's head. The boy's parents woke up the next morning and found him unconscious with a large unexplained bump on his head. Clary never confessed.

Elizabeth withdrew Clary from school and hired a private tutor. Marcus found a job that kept him from the house most of the day. Clary thrived at home. She learned, and she spent time outside when she could. Marcus avoided her, and Elizabeth overcompensated.

Then a couple years later, a miracle.

Marcus came home at three in the afternoon, hours earlier than usual, and dropped his briefcase on the kitchen counter. He dismissed the tutor and called Elizabeth. He found the answer to their problem, and they could be a real family again.

Elizabeth rushed home to see her husband sitting next to her daughter, and her heart melted at the rare sight. She would listen. Whatever he suggested, she would at least listen. Elizabeth longed to be the family they were once upon a time.

Marcus billed for several hospitals, and consultants passed through they're office like a revolving door. They checked dates, codes, and times. Marcus happened to have a new hospital on his books, and the consultant came in to discuss coding. They wanted a slightly different system. No names used. Numbers were more efficient. Only the hard drive on the main server kept names. None of the billing needed them. Simply a paperwork issue. Marcus didn't care. He'd give them whatever they wanted.

The consultant was mid-forties with short brown hair, medium build, glasses, dressed in a nice brown suit. Forgettable after a first glance. He carried a briefcase of the same color. No jewelry, but Marcus noticed his cuff links. They reflected the office lights. Gold and engraved with "SL."

"Pleasure to meet you, Mr. Clay. I'm Steve Larson. I've brought you the key to our coding. You'll memorize it. We don't use names as we have sensitive procedures, and we respect our patients' privacy to the utmost. We deal in, uh, special cases."

"Plastic surgery?" Marcus smiled.

Steve laughed. "Not quite, but I'm sure you have some of those, too." He shook his head and lowered his voice. "More special." He looked around. "Our patients are gifted, Mr. Clay."

Marcus frowned. "Gifted? I don't understand."

"We have a young woman who can move small things," Steve paused, "with her mind."

"No way." Marcus narrowed his eyes. "People can't really do those things, can they?"

"Can and do, Mr. Clay." Steve tapped his folder. "Some are born with abilities that humble the rest."

Marcus glanced at the folder. "Sunmos Lab?"

"Indeed." Steve's brown eyes studied him. "Why?"

"I have a daughter." Marcus glanced around.

"Mr. Clay." Steve's voice was placating. "I'm sure your daughter is special, but these children have abilities."

Marcus cleared his throat. "She can walk in your dreams."

CHAPTER 3

Elizabeth looked at the pamphlet in front of her. It was trifold and spoke of a wonderful in-house facility where special children could finally have their needs met one-on-one with dedicated staff. No longer would these children be afflicted with guilt over their abilities, they would learn to hone and use their gifts for good. Medical staff available 24/7. Scholarships available for patients in need.

"There are others?" She set the pamphlet down and stared at Marcus.

"I couldn't believe it, either." He pointed to the pamphlet. "Steve pulled one of these out of his briefcase and told me all about the place. It's here, in Oklahoma. Well, it's way out in the sticks, but they need the privacy for the patients. He made it sound like more states have these facilities, but I don't care about them." Marcus put his hand over Elizabeth's. "Clary can go to a real school for children like her."

"No." Clary glared at both her parents. "I don't want to go. I want to stay here."

"Honey, we haven't even looked at this place." Elizabeth tucked a red curl behind her daughter's ear. "This facility may be able to help you. And there are other kids who can do neat things, too."

"Neat things?" Marcus glanced at his daughter. "She does invasive things, Liz. Maybe they can teach her not to."

"Daddy doesn't like me, anymore." Clary's eye filled with tears, and she leaned into her mother and sobbed.

Elizabeth patted Clary on the back and glared at Marcus. "Daddy loves you, Clary. We both love you. We're going to go this weekend and look at this school, okay?" She kissed Clary's forehead. She hoped it was the answer to all her prayers.

****

They drove two hours to a patch of land outside Bells, Oklahoma. It was in the east-central part of the state, and pavement was as rare as well-done steak. The family bounced the better part of thirty miles before they found solace on a paved road that led to a gated property.

"Has to be it." Marcus checked his phone. No signal. He strained his eyes. "Looks like a big white building back a bit." He honked his horn.

Two men, dressed all in black, walked out from the foliage to the car. They approached Marcus, and he rolled down his window.

"Hi. I'm Marcus Clay and family. We have an appointment with Dr. Hamilton." He handed his license to one of the men. They were both built like bodyguards in jeans and grey t-shirts.

"Drive straight down to the hospital. He's expecting you." The man returned his license, and Marcus nodded his thanks and waited for the gate to open.

They drove slowly and admired the white and grey buildings on each side. Everything appeared neat and tidy.

"Look at how much room you have!" Elizabeth glanced back at Clary who glared out the window.

"It's dusty, and everything is grey."

"The car is kicking up dust, Clary. Give it a chance." Marcus glanced in the rearview mirror. She looked up at him and nodded.

They reached the top of the hill and could finally see what they'd been missing. The facility sat on ten acres surrounded by trees. It was a squat white building with four automatic doors leading in.

Staff parked on the west side under an awning that ran half the length of the building.

"Wow." Marcus backed in under the awning and looked around. "Brand new facility." He shut off the car and turned to his family. "You ready?"

Both ladies exited the opposite side and stood by the car. There was no movement outside. No wind. Even the birds stayed silent.

"Daddy," Clary whispered with eyes wide.

"Mr. Clay and family!"

Clary shrieked.

They all jumped.

"Clary!" Marcus scolded her. He turned back to the man in front of him. "I'm sorry. She's a little high-strung."

"She isn't." Elizabeth glanced at Marcus and then the man in front of them. "I'm Elizabeth Clay. You are?"

"Dr. Arthur Hamilton. Pleased to meet you." He smiled. "Please come inside. We've been looking forward to your visit." He ushered them into the sterile hallway and stopped. "We have our other patients in their rooms right now. Outsiders tend to upset most of them. We are acclimating them to their abilities slowly. As they gain control, we will begin to add other variables."

Clary studied the doctor with the light blue eyes. He wasn't as big as her dad, but he was taller. She didn't like his thin lips or the way he kept clearing his throat. His hands were long, hairy, and he had dirty fingernails. Didn't doctors wash their hands? The doctor looked down at her and then put his hands in his coat pockets.

"I don't like the way it smells here." Clary wrinkled her nose. Something sharp made her eyes water. Did all hospitals smell like this?

"It's bleach, Clary. To keep it clean." Her dad smiled down at her. "It's a good smell."

Doctor Hamilton nodded. "We don't want anyone sick." He smiled. "The hospital is u-shaped. All residents are on the left side, and we have art, music, and activities on the right. We also take our residents out when weather permits and let them enjoy the grounds. It's gorgeous in spring and fall."

"You have academics? Clary won't fall behind in school? She's only six, but she's bright." Elizabeth glanced around.

"Residents have school three days a week. Since it's concentrated here, they don't need five. Tutors work with each child to ensure no student is left behind. We value education here." Doctor Hamilton escorted them to the end of the hall. "Our cafeteria holds all of our residents, but many choose to have quiet time in their room for meals. As I've said, they're adjusting, and we don't want to push them at any point."

"How many residents do you have?"

"Nine right now." Doctor Hamilton motioned back down the hall. "We have room for fifteen. Clary will make ten."

"I realize it covers everything, Doctor Hamilton, but the tuition is a bit pricey." Elizabeth looked at Marcus because they planned for her to make this point. Her husband nodded.

"Oh, my dear Clays. I'm sorry I didn't say anything at the beginning of the tour." Doctor Hamilton removed some papers from his interior jacket pocket. He handed them to Elizabeth with a smile. "Clary received one of our scholarships. There will be no financial burden on your family."

Elizabeth took the papers and looked through them, perplexed. "When did we apply for this?"

"I did." Marcus appeared sheepish. "I'm sorry, honey. It was a long shot, but I thought maybe we would get it, and I knew it would help." He kissed his wife on the cheek. "Isn't it great?"

Doctor Hamilton nodded. "Everything is contingent, of course, on Clary being able to do what you say she can do." He peered down at Clary as if she were a bug.

Clary felt all hope die at the looks on her parents' faces. This place thought of everything.

Elizabeth turned to her daughter and squatted down beside her. "Clary. How would you like to go to school here with other children that have abilities? Children who understand what it's like to be different?"

"I'd rather keep my tutor," Clary whispered to her mother.

"Oh, love." Elizabeth pulled Clary to her and hugged her tight. "I know change is scary, but your tutor can't help you with your gift. She can only help with school. This place can help you with all parts of you." She looked up at Doctor Hamilton. "And we're allowed to visit?"

"Any time you want." He nodded.

"I don't want you away from me, Clary, but I don't want to hold you back, either." Elizabeth kissed her cheek. "I love you more than anything. Can you please try it here? Maybe for a month?"

Clary sighed and looked into her mother's eyes, so much like her own. "Yes, Mama."

Elizabeth pulled her in for another tight hug. "That's my girl." She straightened. "We'd like to give this place a try, Doctor Hamilton, perhaps for a month or two?"

"Ah, Mrs. Clay. We aim to please."

****

Clary watched her parents fill out more forms, and her stomach dropped when they signed the last. She knew Daddy didn't like her but not why. He would probably be happy she was here. But Mama? Clary fought back tears as she said goodbye to them from her new room. Doctor Hamilton said it was best for everyone. He had someone go get her belongings from the car and bring them to her new room. She already hated him. Daddy thought ahead to bring her things.

Clary sat on her bed by the two suitcases and looked out her window at the trees. Alone. The sun sank slowly, and she knew she would not sleep. Had she ever slept in any besides her own? No. Now, she sat on a small hard bed in a strange new place. It couldn't be much worse.

CHAPTER 4

"You think we did the right thing, don't you?" Elizabeth's light green eyes, the mirror of her daughter's, were worried.

"My love. I know we did." Marcus kissed her forehead. "Clary will thrive there. They know exactly what to do with a girl like her. You heard them. They're experts. She's in good hands."

Elizabeth let her head fall on her husband's chest. "I hope so," she murmured.

****

Early the next morning, Steve Larson hand-delivered a check to Marcus Clay for three million dollars. Marcus cashed the check and was out of town by the time Elizabeth sat down to eat lunch. When she arrived home that evening, his "Dear John" letter sat up straight against the salt and pepper shakers on the kitchen counter.

First, the pain at his betrayal of their marriage, and then fury he'd given their daughter away and then left. Elizabeth swore she'd retrieve Clary the next day. Forget Marcus Clay and the disgusting piece of shit he was.

Elizabeth dressed early the next morning and walked into the kitchen. She needed lots of coffee and some toast to settle her stomach. She pulled her hair back into a bun on her head and wore a pantsuit in grey silk. Nothing would stop her. She put two pieces of bread in the toaster and grabbed her coffee.

The doorbell rang, and she frowned. Neighbor? Paper boy?

Elizabeth opened the door, and her brain registered the threat too late. The stranger threw liquid into her face, and she screamed as it burned her eyes and dripped down her face. Elizabeth opened her mouth to scream again when it splashed across her chest and down her right arm and hand. She was on fire!

"Help me! I'm dying! Help me! I'm on fire!" Elizabeth rubbed her face and body while she screamed and tried to get it off her until she fell and knew no more.

****

Pain.

Exquisite pain.

Darkness.

She couldn't...breathe.

She moaned and cried while hands held her down.

Please.

Please.

Make it stop.

Pain.

****

"Miss Lizzie. You awake?"

Elizabeth swallowed, which hurt, and whispered, "Yes. Why is it dark? My voice?"

"Oh, child. You're one of those. Have to know everything right away." The voice sighed. "I'm Nurse Verna. Here to take care of you." Elizabeth felt a soft hand cover hers. "I'm going to tell you the same way you asked, child. The same exact way." Verna paused. "You're blind. Chemicals blinded you, darlin'. Those same chemicals? Some got in those lungs of yours. And to top your shitshow off, pardon my language, your right arm and hand sustained damage, too."

Tears slid from Elizabeth's eyes. "Blind?" She reached up and touched her face. Cloth covered her eyes.

"You won't be taking those bandages off until doc says so, Miss Lizzie." Verna dabbed at her tears. "Now, your left hand is fine. I don't know if you're one or the other hand, but it wouldn't hurt to start practicing with that one."

"Practice what?" Elizabeth's hoarse voice strained as she struggled to sit up. "The fucking piano? Surgery?" She collapsed back against her pillow and breathed shallowly in and out.

"Don't you hyperventilate on me, child."

"Hy-hy-hyper…" Elizabeth hit the bed with her left hand. Then again. Then…darkness.

****

"I know you're awake, child."

Elizabeth tried to pull her thoughts together. The pain pushed them away, but she fought to keep them. "My daughter," she whispered.

"You have a daughter?"

"Yes." Elizabeth smiled. She would find her daughter and get her back.

"I'll ask. Doesn't say anything in your records. You're a widow with no children."

"No." Panic built in her chest. "Wrong."

"Child. I do not want to strap you down, and I don't want to drug you. Calm down. Let me check on this for you."

"Please." Elizabeth reached out for Verna's hand. "Please."

Nurse Verna checked which set off bells that would rather remain silent. Elizabeth Clay found herself on a cocktail of drugs that kept her a bit hazy on details and moved to an assisted living center with Nurse Verna. A trust paid the bills. A trust from the three million Marcus took since his dead body was found two weeks later with a bullet between the eyes in a shallow grave in Texas.

CHAPTER 5

Rissa hissed at the nearest doctor and tossed her long-matted scarlet hair. He scrambled back with his hands up, and Rissa grinned.

"Fucking scaredy cat." The grin held nothing but malice for the recipients. Light green eyes scanned the room and focused on the two doctors and one nurse hiding behind full-body protective suits and masks. They tranquilized and trussed her up. Rissa once refused to eat for days. They strapped her to the bed and force fed her. It was a miserable and embarrassing time. She finally gave in to the inevitable. She looked at all her food with suspicion daily. This time, the fucking meatloaf did her in.

"Love how you poison me so I can do your dirty work." Rissa bared her teeth. "Why don't you come out of those fucking suits, and we can play?" She studied the taller doctor. "I only want to walk through your mind, Dr. Bennett." The suit moved slightly, and Rissa hid her triumph behind a small laugh. "Pull a few cords. Open a few boxes. Leave you drooling like a lobotomy patient for say, the next forty or so years of your life, you evil fuck."

"Put the weapon on the table."

Rissa locked herself tight. Shut herself down as best she could. *The weapon*. These bastards used her as one and returned her to her case afterwards. Never mind the cost.

The two guards grabbed and shoved her face down on the hospital bed. She wore faded scrubs. They'd dressed her in a hospital gown for years, with no thought to her modesty. Rissa had to beg for the scrubs she currently wore. Threadbare and soft, they were one of only two pair she owned. She wouldn't beg again. She needed to escape here before they sucked the life out of her like a child's juice box and tossed her remains in the trash.

The guards flipped her over and stared down at her. They also wore full protective gear, and Rissa could not even detect eye color. She could only see her pale face reflected back at her. She already looked dead.

"Be still," commanded the voice close to her feet. "I will have them break your arms if you fight. You know the rules."

Indeed. The damnable rules. Rissa lay still while the guards, one on each side, cuffed her wrists to the sides of the hospital bed. There was no room to move. They belted her ankles to the bottom half of the bed tight enough to cut off her circulation.

Rissa fought hard when she turned eleven, convinced she moved quicker than those in suits and could run before they could catch her. She bucked up against the guards that day, and the one on her left snapped her arm without pause. Rissa screamed as the pain shot through her, and the guard cuffed her, the same as always, to the bed. They made her finish her mission before they gave her the smallest of pain meds and set the bone.

One guard stepped away quickly, but the one on her right stayed a second longer. "When they're done with you, little bitch, you and I are gonna have some fun just like this." He moved to join his buddy.

Rissa's face didn't change a bit, but she filed away the voice. Chet, if she weren't mistaken. The one who broke her arm without pause. There were six guards, and they brought them all in secretly so she never saw them. The guards were supposed to be careful. They were told Rissa was a dangerous woman. But some were lazy. She loved the lazy ones.

"Doctors…" the voice trailed off.

The trio moved from the walls and toward her. Rissa closed her eyes. She refused to be a part of this as much as she could. They didn't have her permission. They never had.

"Strap the chin down."

Rissa fought the claustrophobia that welled in her chest. She eased her breath slowly in and out of her lungs. If they knew how much it upset her, they would use this simple fact to torture her. One more tool in their toolbox to break her.

"Pulse spiked." A pause. "Now normal."

"Insert the IV."

Rissa didn't give a shit about needles. These places stabbed her incessantly to drug her, or to take blood from her. Her arms looked like a junkie's. The bruises never healed. It was, as everything else, a pain on top of another pain, forever.

No warning as the needle slid deep in her flesh. They never covered her eyes as the color changed when she went deep. They always checked her. Rissa kept her tears, as she'd been keeping them for nearly a decade. Fuck them, she thought to herself. Fuck them all...as she drifted off.

****

TJ Hightower liked to say he was a cowboy first and politician second. Didn't stop him from raking in old money from surrounding ranchers while bending over whichever direction he needed for the new money.

TJ wanted a seat in the Governor's house without a care of how to get there. Young thirties. Married five years. White as goose shit. Big oil and lobbyists were practically making money for him. Start small. Build up that base. Move up the political ladder. Have a couple kids. Make sure that others knew he was available to chat. Sure, he had a few mishaps in his youth. Hell, that was expected in Oklahoma. But he was young, white, and willing to say whatever they needed.

Except, TJ moved way ahead of himself. Fancy parties and

fundraising brought a lot of new people into his life. A lot of new women. And TJ thought himself a man among men. Except, men didn't like other men fucking their wives. They really took exception to a married man bedding their daughters.

TJ Hightower sat in his living room with the lights low. The moon shone in through the French doors leading to the pool. He wore boxers and a T-shirt with the current Governor's picture on it that proclaimed, "If bullshit were music, he'd have a brass band!" He sipped two fingers of old whiskey and leaned back to relax.

Sarah visited her mother for a week this time of year, and he loved the quiet house. No yelling at him for not putting his pants in the basket or leaving a razor on the sink or God knows what else she wanted to nag on him.

He rolled his eyes and took another sip. Everything slipped into place when you had your shit together.

"Did it? Did it really?"

TJ jumped and spilled his drink. He glared at the person beside him on the couch. "I don't know who in the fuck you are, but you need to leave before I call the police."

Rissa yawned. "Boring."

He put his drink on the table. "I'm warning you."

"I'm warning you." Rissa motioned for him to sit back, and he did. "I see a young idiot who didn't know to keep it in his pants. You know, only for wifely events."

TJ tried to sit up but couldn't. "Who are you?"

"It doesn't matter, TJ. I'm here to kill you. Would you like to know why? Or do you simply want to die in ignorance?"

"I don't want to die." TJ's eyes filled with fear.

"Too late, bro." Rissa stood and sighed. "What makes you think you can keep doing the same shitty things daily, and it's going to be okay? Treating your wife like shit and fucking anything that looks at you?" She walked to the French doors. "I only get to see this shit when I'm killing people." Rissa touched the glass. "How fucked up is that?" She turned. "You have this every day, and you're out fucking the wives and daughters of your so-called friends." She paused. "So you know, it was the daughters that did you in."

"What?" TJ stared at her.

"Close your mouth; you look like a guppy." Rissa felt time closing in. It pissed her off as it always did. She sat back on the couch. "Jerry Bond's daughter? The sixteen-year-old one? Bad call. Loretta Swan's seventeen-year-old daughter? Same. Those weren't yours to have. And now someone has decided the world would be a much better place without you."

Tears streaked down TJ's cheeks. "Please. Don't kill me! My wife? Sarah? She won't be able to survive without me! And a crime scene will be too much for her. Please!"

Rissa blinked and then laughed. "Shut the fuck up. We both know you're not altruistic. Besides, TJ, some people who are really smart paid some incredibly fucked-up people to drug me and kill you in your dream. Isn't that the absolute limit?" She smiled. "Now. I'm going to come a little bit closer and scramble the fuck out of your grey matter."

TJ screamed.

Rissa put her fingers on his temple and ignored the man's outburst. "Now, be a good boy." Her light green eyes darkened to a deep blue.

CHAPTER 6

Rissa's sessions, as she called them, gave her a small boost. She acted the opposite for her captors. She stayed in bed that day and ate everything they made. Cook doubled the portions for energy. The staff preferred her either drugged or dreaming. She treasured these moments that were hers alone.

She kept her eyes closed when her door opened. They never did back-to-back sessions, and it wasn't even two yet. Rissa wanted her quiet back.

"You're awake." Bennett spoke with no inflection.

"You know I am." Rissa opened her eyes to look at the interloper. "What do you want?" She made a show of yawning loudly.

"You played with your prey last night and took too long. It's unnecessary."

"You're not giving me a fucking grape sucker?" Rissa sat up quickly, and the suit moved back. It raised an arm up with a cattle prod sizzling in her face.

"You fuckers and your electric toys." Rissa hissed and grabbed the prod with her left hand. It sizzled and burned against her flesh.

"Stop!" He pushed her hand away. "Jesus Christ! Are you fucking crazy!" Bennett turned and left the room while two medics rushed in to bandage her hand.

"Can't have a defective weapon, can you?" Rissa screamed. She watched the two medics bandage her left hand with little interest. Until she saw it and quickly looked away. One of the medics had to be new. She hadn't taped her wrists as tight as she should. One glance. Rissa locked it and hid it in her mind. A pink and green beaded bracelet with the name "Mandy" in the middle.

They finished and left the room quickly. Rissa's hand throbbed, and she lay back on her bed. She rested her left arm on her chest. *Mandy*? The medic's name? Sister? Daughter? Mother? Rissa closed her eyes. She didn't let herself dream. Not yet. There were pieces left to gather.

Rissa lived at this facility for nearly a decade. A decade of pricks, and needles, ha ha, and death. They didn't come for her every night, but there were weeks they made the Grim Reaper a busy fellow. They kept her as a weapon, an asset, but also a liability.

They found out when she turned nine, she was able to take a piece of someone she had simply seen and dream walk in them.

It was at the first facility.

Rissa sat in the chair by her window and colored a page for her mother. The doctor assured her that even though her mother couldn't visit, he would mail the page to her. Rissa worked extra hard to make it look nice. She didn't bother coloring one for her father.

She remembered reaching for the green crayon when she heard Matt, one of the nurses, below her window. Rissa reached out to close the window before Matt lit the usual cigarette. The smoke wafted directly into her room. His words stopped her.

"Doc Hamilton is a real sonofabitch." A pause. Must be talking on the phone. Rissa dropped her hands and sat back. She rarely heard profanity, and Matt sounded mad.

"It's great money." Matt sighed and then lowered his voice. Rissa strained toward the window. "You don't understand, Ma. There are six kids here. Five kids with no families." Another pause. "No families because Hamilton took care of them so he could have the kids. Yeah. They're a little dangerous, but they're kids, Ma!"

Quiet. "I don't know..." Matt's voice trailed off as he walked away from Rissa's window.

Rissa frowned. Hamilton took care of her mother? What did that mean? She put the green crayon down and pushed away from the small desk. Fear bit at her and made her stomach hurt. Did he put her mama in a small room, too? Lock her away from Rissa so they couldn't see each other? Had Doctor Hamilton been lying to her? Fury overrode fear as Rissa pictured her mama sad in a small room. Oh, no. Rissa would take care of Doctor Hamilton.

****

Rissa could will herself to sleep, but the doctors left nothing to chance. They drugged her every time. They needed complete control. There was a small window to go and come back. She only failed twice. But they cut her food intake in half and stripped her room for a week. Rissa never failed again.

They led her to the hospital bed in the room with the doctor windows. She could see nameless faces up above as they stared down at her. Rissa wanted to scream at them and ask where her mother was, but she bided her time. She would dream walk and find her own answer.

A nurse slid an IV into her arm, and Rissa winced. Two doctors came into the room and flanked her. She looked up into ice-blue eyes, Hamilton. She didn't recognize the other with light brown eyes.

"It's an important day, Rissa. We have other doctors around the world who have come to see you and your abilities. We're going to have two scenes. Isn't that exciting?" Dr. Hamilton's eyes narrowed in warning.

Rissa nodded.

"Wonderful!" Dr. Hamilton turned to the gallery above. "The patient will be under longer than usual. There will be two targets this time. The patient will be administered the drug in approximately one minute. Set your watches." He walked to the wall under the gallery, and the other doctor followed him.

Rissa lay incredibly still. She used the drug a little bit, but she stayed in control. All the scientific geniuses never felt the need to adjust the dosage with her body weight. Truthfully, it hadn't changed a great deal, but she still acted like the smallest dose put her out. The drug entered her body, and she floated away.

****

Rissa sat on the edge of the inside pool while her legs dangled in the warm water. She wore her hospital gown and underwear. The sun peeked through the outside windows. It appeared to be late afternoon. She looked around. Nobody else in the area. Rissa frowned and stood up. Usually, they wanted her to deflate a decorated floatie and throw it in the pool. Then make sure it sank to the bottom. *Odd.*

Rissa walked through the sliding doors into the kitchen. Two plastic blow-up people sat in chairs at the small light wooden table. They were naked. Rissa grimaced when she realized she could see everything on both. These weren't floaties. They were gross. She looked at the table top. A large knife lay in the middle, and Rissa glanced at it and then the plastic people. She went to work.

Pieces of plastic people exploded over the entire kitchen. Once Rissa started, she couldn't stop. She didn't want one piece to be able to be used to identify what either was. Plastic confetti decorated the table and floor. She also needed a bit more time. Finally, Rissa threw the knife back on the table and nodded in approval. Now. For real business.

The scene morphed into a sad brown living room with Dr. Hamilton on a sad light brown couch. Rissa walked over and sat down.

"What are you doing here?" Hamilton demanded. He wore a brown shirt and brown slacks. His light blue eyes furious.

Rissa looked around and frowned. "This isn't my second scene?" She allowed herself the smallest of smiles. "You must have been so busy this last week preparing for this show. How lucky for me you feel safe enough to take a little power nap. Isn't that what you call them?"

"You little bitch. Go do your job," he ordered.

"I have questions."

Dr. Hamilton's hand came up, and Rissa stopped it with a thought. "Not going to work here, doc. Now. Back to my questions." She turned to him and stared him in the eye. "Where is my mama?"

"Gone," he bit out. "Never coming back."

"What did you do to her?" Rissa reached out as if to put her fingers on his forehead.

"Nothing! She left. Left you and skipped town. I swear!" Sweat rolled down Dr. Hamilton's face.

Rissa pushed past the pain at his words. "Why am I here? What am I really doing?"

"Rissa." Doc Hamilton's voice softened. "You are helping us with difficult people who have secrets. We're training you to step inside their heads and find those secrets."

"I destroy. I don't find." Rissa frowned. "I shredded two plastic people for my first target. Why?"

A pause. "You're young, but you have to be prepared if the target is naked. We didn't want to shock you."

Rissa grimaced. "Well. I didn't like it."

Dr. Hamilton raised his voice. "Rissa! Enough of this nonsense. Go find your next target right this minute. You're wasting time, and the other doctors will be disappointed."

"Funny thing." Rissa leaned forward and pressed her fingers to

Hamilton's temple. Her clear green eyes turned icy blue. She moved their bodies to the roof of doc's building with a simple thought. Rissa made him step up on the nearest edge and look down. His legs shook.

"Rissa! Stop this!"

She walked to him and swung her legs over the side. She sat beside him. "I'm pretty smart for nine, doc." Rissa raised her face to the sun. "I don't think you're making me do good things. I don't even think you like good things. I don't know what you did to my mama, but you did something. I can feel it as sure as the breeze on my face."

"Rissa," Hamilton begged.

She sighed and looked up at him. "That's another thing. I think you're having me hurt people, doc. And if that's true..." she trailed off and smiled up at him, "...then I should have some say in who I hurt."

Rissa pushed Dr. Hamilton's legs as hard as she could. They buckled, and he made a sound of surprise as he pitched forward between the buildings toward the dark alley below. She had a few seconds of satisfaction before the screams started.

CHAPTER 7

Rissa woke quickly and sat up in her hospital bed. She glanced over where Dr. Hamilton last stood and admired the pile of broken bones and slushy flesh. Rissa didn't regret pushing the sadist off his apartment building. She stayed at his facility for more than two years. Two years of pinches and slaps. Two years of punishments for nothing she did. And the lies. The lies. Fury beat in her chest, but she soothed it down as a child to a bird knocked from its nest. Smoothed the feathers one-by-one.

She watched two orderlies scoop the good doctor up and wheel him out. No one seemed to even notice her. Rissa glanced up at the doctor gallery. Gone. Nurses swept and swabbed the floor by the walls. Murmurs and weeping. Mourning a man who didn't deserve it. They cleaned up the mess and left out the same door they came in.

"Feel better?"

Rissa's head snapped toward the shadows.

The doctor with the brown eyes emerged. He had a clipboard tucked under his arm. Shorter than Doc Hamilton. Harder voice.

"I'm tired." Rissa crossed her legs and closed her eyes.

"Murder makes you tired?"

She kept her eyes closed. "I'm a child. I don't murder people."

"Did you push him in front of a car?" The doctor tapped his pen on the clipboard. "Have a gang beat him up?" More tapping. "That man died a horrific death because he pissed you off."

Rissa opened her eyes and glared at the doctor. "Did it ever occur to you maybe he deserved it?"

"I know he deserved it, Rissa." The doctor walked up to her hospital bed and stared at her with a look she didn't recognize.

"But how did you feel when you did it?"

She knew what he wanted, almost begged for with that question. Rissa looked up at him with big green eyes and pig tails in her red hair. "Remorse."

"You're sorry?" he prompted.

"Yes." She nodded with no expression on her face. "Sorry I could only do it once."

****

Sheer childhood stupidity made Rissa believe her life couldn't be any worse than it was with Dr. Hamilton. That was a lie. It was the biggest lie.

The doctor with the brown eyes drugged and moved her to another facility. They settled her into a locked room with a bed and toilet. No mirrors or windows. No crayons or things to color. The walls as white as her tired flesh.

Rissa woke with a raging headache and pressed her hands to her temples. The smell of bleach and ammonia stung her nostrils.

"We weren't sure about dosage. May have used a bit much."

She squinted against the bright light and looked toward the voice she recognized. "Where am I?"

"Your new home. Brand new facility with all the bells and whistles. State of the art alarm system. Protective suits for all staff." He chuckled. "We don't want any repeat performances. Probably best we don't give you any ammunition."

Rissa made herself listen to every word. She thought she'd been in hell. Drugged and slapped. Forced to perform on command.

Anger lit in her belly, a comfort in her hollowed-out body. She made eye contact with the brown-eyed doctor who now covered up every piece of himself.

He gasped and then gave himself a little shake. "I don't ever want to be on the other side of those eyes." He jotted something on the clipboard and then settled it under his left leg and leaned forward. "You're full of rage, Red. It's sweeter than any honey and more bitter than the darkest chocolate."

The doctor stood. "Keep doing your job, and we'll be fine. Stop doing your job? You'll find out what real punishment is." He scooped the chair and clipboard with one hand and left.

Rissa watched the door close, and then she looked around the room. A camera above the door to watch her. She stood on shaking legs and walked into a small room with a toilet and a sink. Rissa didn't see a camera, but she didn't trust any of them.

They would watch her use the toilet, like a caged mouse shitting in the corner. She turned the water on and splashed some on her face. Then she cupped her hands and took a long drink. Rissa wiped her hands on her gown and walked back to bed. She covered up with the light sheet and shut her eyes.

****

Rissa's new normal sucked more than the old normal. Two guards escorted her from her room to another massive room with a hospital bed. Two doctors and a nurse. Strapped down. Needle in her arm. Talisman of the target. Destroy target. Shuffled back to room.

The facility continued her "education", if one could call it that. Old tapes about reading and math she could watch if she asked for them. Promptly removed after viewed. Rissa learned to glean information from targets. They became her educators.

For the first few years, Rissa would wander around the environment of the target. She would eyeball the talisman and know it held a life. Male. Female. It held no clue to her. But the surroundings fascinated her.

One room filled with golf clubs, balls, and flags. Another room filled with candles. Another filled with ancient knives. Rissa knew the facility didn't control the environment. Either the target or she did. But which?

Could she create the environment into anything she desired? What *did* she desire? Rissa wanted soft things. She experimented the two years with imposing her will on her surroundings.

Then she turned eleven.

CHAPTER 8

When Doc Brown Eyes brought Rissa to the new lab, he made a more secure cage. No windows. Single story. And a nice low vibrational hum all day and night that put Rissa off her game.

Everything vibrates at a certain frequency. The hum acted as an electronic security gate. Rissa couldn't reach outside of it to enter anyone's dreams. It was white noise in her head whenever she tried to mentally escape. Ten seconds in, she wanted to pull her own eyeballs out. The pain made a migraine feel like nothing.

Rissa knew she couldn't use anything from the outside world to escape. She decided to use what she knew from the inside.

Doc Brown Eyes hired six guards. There were three doctors. Three nurses. Four medics who rotated twelve-hour shifts. Cook. Rissa assumed they paid an outside company for biohazard disposal. There must also be at least one person above the crew who they reported all their information.

But let's stick to the here and now.

Rissa fought hard for four years before she began to plan. She suffered bone breaks, beatings, and humiliations from ages nine to thirteen. The dream of a simple escape born and died hundreds of times in hundreds of ways before she accepted the truth. "Easy" would never be a part of her life.

Each staff became a number. Each number a piece of the puzzle. Each piece of the puzzle needed to complete her escape.

First, she ruled out staff she knew she could never access. Doc Brown Eyes and Safe Space Doc fit the bill. Safe Space Doc was the voice in the lab next to the big room with the hospital bed she renamed Hell Hall. But Doctor Bennett? Rissa wanted him. She needed someone with full access, and she scared him. Bonus.

Rissa needed one nurse. They were all loyal to the doctors and treated her as they would a prisoner, cautious and careful. The nurse might be harder than the doctor.

A set of security guards. Next to impossible. They shielded themselves mentally and physically. Rissa knew this would take time. If she focused on a pair of guards, and then they left, she would have to start all over. What did she have but time, though?

One medic. Rissa needed access to her medical charts. They could be slowly killing her, for all she knew. She needed to peek at her medical info. See what the doctors and nurses saw.

What would they do if she escaped?

Hunt her down like a dog? Kill her to hide their secrets? Could it be any worse than staying?

No.

****

Rissa started her escape plan when she turned thirteen. It seemed a favorable age. She set her parameters of not killing children to the doctors and began her lessons of observation. They dismissed her rule and placed her on the hospital bed. She paid attention to the smallest detail.

The room nurse could barely fasten the chin strap. She was short. Good. Rissa finished her assignment, and a guard escorted her back to her room. Tall. Broad. He opened her bedroom door and closed it behind. Good.

Rissa made her mental notes.

A few minutes later the other guard brought her tray in. Tall. Slender. Rissa took her time eating the turkey sandwich and chips. The guard looked around the room a couple of times. She smiled as she took a bite. This one grew bored easily. Good.

Day in. Day out.

Rissa killed. Rissa planned.

When she was fourteen, Hell Hall nurse didn't pull her glove up all the way, and Rissa touched her bare skin. It took everything in her to remain calm. Rissa had her. She waited impatiently to be escorted to her room. She inhaled her food, complained of a headache, and lay in her bed.

Rissa felt electric. She hoped the one touch would give her the power to supersede the electronic frequency surrounding her. A direct line had to work.

But what if it didn't?

She would find another way. There had to be another way.

Dark came slowly. Her last mission took place in the wee hours of the morning. Rissa didn't want to take the risk of trying to enter the nurse's dream and hitting a brick wall. She needed to be sure.

When her body told her it was after midnight, Rissa closed her eyes and dreamt.

****

Sherri Rhodes slept comfortably in her California king with a periwinkle silk nightgown down to her thighs and her light brown hair in soft curls around her relaxed face. Sky blue satin sheets lay in waves on the bed.

Rissa studied her. She thought the nurse would be older. Rissa walked over and touched the sheets on the bed and rubbed them between her fingers and thumb. They slid through and fell back on the bed. Had Rissa ever felt anything as soft?

Did Rissa pay for all this? She glanced around the room at the large dresser and larger television on the wall. She walked through an open doorway into a luxurious bathroom in pastel greens, blues, and peach. There was a large circular tub on the back wall with steps leading to it and knobs on the side Rissa didn't understand. On her right was a large shower with rock as the sides and two shower heads with a clear sliding door.

Anger boiled deep. Rissa tried to push it down. Yet, everywhere she looked was a testament to her pain and another's pleasure at the cost of it.

Another needle mark? Another set of satin sheets. Strapped down again? Luxury bath towels.

Bile filled Rissa's throat, and she woke before she threw up on herself. She barely made it to the bathroom before retching. She hugged the toilet as her legs shook. Rissa heaved again, and nothing came up but stomach bile.

She felt herself moved backwards as a cool wash cloth was placed on her forehead. Rissa closed her eyes as she was half carried/dragged to her bed and placed on the mattress.

They took her vitals and blood. Rissa heard the door close and exhaled. She hoped she was done for the night.

The door opened once more. "What happened?"

Rissa wondered briefly if she could will herself to die. And then realized she'd already be dead if that were the case.

"Didn't feel good." Rissa kept her eyes closed.

Doc Brown Eyes tapped his clipboard. "Out of nowhere?"

"Yes." She heard papers rustle.

"You didn't eat anything after lunch. You need to eat every meal. I'll add in snacks."

"Great. Fresh fruit, while you're at it." Rissa opened one eye to study him. "Go away. They took my blood. I'm sure they'll let you know if I'm dying." She closed her eye and sighed.

"They'll bring you a tray in five minutes. You need to eat some of it." A command. No love lost. Afraid the weapon may be malfunctioning. The door closed.

Fuuuuuuuuuuuucccccccccckkkkkkk

True to his word, a tray arrived. A medic, not a guard, delivered it.

Rissa made herself sit up as the medic removed the lid. She had been flippant about the fresh fruit, but there were grapes, oranges, and strawberries next to three pancakes, milk, and two eggs. Her stomach growled.

She made short work of the food, and the medic took the tray and left. Rissa closed her eyes and reached out. Nearly five in the morning. Well, that first foray into Sherri's dreams did a number on her.

Rissa knew her naiveté would cost her in the real world. But it would only cost her soft things, and she didn't need soft things. She thought of Sherri's sheets. Sherri strapped a child down and shoved a needle in her arm any time someone told her to for those soft sheets. Sherri could go fuck herself. She valued those sheets over Rissa's life.

Rissa thought she'd seen so many awful things, but they only kept coming. They didn't stop. She would have to be harder. Tougher. Make herself into someone who didn't act like anything hurt her. Don't react to the insults and slurs. *I'm a weapon*, she thought. *Be the weapon.*

****

Rissa became proficient at the kill and worked her time clock. She would focus on her target and use them to find things out before punching their time card. As long as her eyes stayed the target's color, she was safe. Rissa learned everything she could about weapons and computers, her two main areas of interest. She would barter with the target for pleasurable ways of dying. Would they rather die by multiple razor blade cuts starting with their genitals? Or would they rather die by sexy assassin? After Rissa explained what the options were, it was unanimous.

Rissa declared she wanted books to read. She didn't particularly care which kind, but her brain rotted daily, and she needed something to keep her mind busy. Doc Brown Eyes acted as if she asked for his computer and password.

"You don't need books."

"Afraid I might get ideas or something?" Rissa looked at him in disbelief. "Give me the fucking classics. I don't care. But I'm tired of counting the spots on these white fucking walls in-between killing people who may or may not deserve it."

Doc Brown Eyes put his hands on his hips. "No books."

She glared. "Get me. Some fucking. Books!"

"You seem to forget all your power is when you're asleep. You're nothing but an underweight needy child when you're awake. More of a liability, really."

"While that may be so," Rissa glared up at him, "I more than earn my keep by killing all the shitty nocturnal targets you give me. How many have I killed for you, doc? Hundreds? Thousands? More than enough for some fucking books!"

"Be careful how you speak to me," he warned in a soft voice. "You are a tool. Nothing more. Remember I only need your brain. You can dream walk with both arms broke. Or maybe four or five fingers?"

Doc Brown Eyes turned and slammed the door behind him.

Rissa flipped the door off and sat back on her bed. She didn't let the scowl on her face slip an inch. She'd play the hard ass as long as needed. The fact Doc Brown Eyes was entirely correct scared her. God forbid they ever find another her. She would be dead within an hour.

Two weeks later, Rissa held "The Three Musketeers" in her hand.

She read the beginning over and over again until it began to make sense. She had no idea how to pronounce any names, but gave nicknames as she went along. Rissa knew asshole doc gave her the book as a joke. It took her over three months to finish, and she loved it.

CHAPTER 9

After Rissa finished her book, she decided to enter Sherri's dream again. She would shut out the luxury and focus on her daily routine at home and the facility. Make the nurse repeat it without realizing Rissa manipulated her and actually stood in the background, watching.

Rissa waited for a non-murder day and ate her entire dinner. She lay back on her bed and closed her eyes. Wait, she told herself. Wait. After midnight. Rissa shifted in her bed and drifted off to sleep.

Sherri slept, once again, with not a care in the world. Rissa stiffened her spine. She checked the alarm clock and set it to go off. Then, she became a shadow. Rissa needed to keep her concentration because now she held both of them in a dream state, and she needed to manipulate Sherri. Everything Sherri saw came from Rissa. Rissa needed to be precise. A false move could wake or warn Sherri.

The alarm went off, and Sherri slapped it with a groan. She rolled out of bed and slid blue slippers on. Rissa brought her hand down, and the scene changed to Sherri in the kitchen. She wore khaki scrubs and blue and peach tennis shoes. She pulled her hair up in a tight bun on her head and sipped coffee. Sherri made an iced coffee and turned…

…to step into her car. Rissa sat, invisible, next to her. Sherri changed the music station, and Rissa cataloged Sherri's location before they drove away. Sherri turned off the car, and Rissa, for the first time in her life, studied the lab from the outside.

The large concrete rectangle sat on an even larger rectangle piece of pavement. They faced the short side as Sherri drove into the parking lot and parked in her normal place. She fussed with her hair a minute and pulled her lanyard from her purse. Sherri hung it around her neck and stepped out of her car. Alarm set. Ready to go.

Rissa followed, literally in Sherri's shadow. Her heart beat quicker than she wanted, but she maintained control of the illusion.

Sherri scanned her card at the first double doors, and they slid open. She looked up into a camera at the second set, and the doors buzzed to let her in. Rissa cursed and followed.

Sherri walked all the way down a long hallway and made a left before the last exit sign. She ducked into a small room with lockers and suits. She put her purse up, walked farther back, and opened another door.

Rissa almost lost her composure. Doc Brown Eyes sat at the white round table in the middle with scrubs, gloves, and face coverings. He showed no bare skin. Rissa knew she was busted.

Sherri laughed. "Never going to know what you look like, am I doc?" She poured herself another cup of coffee. Sherri sipped it and sighed. "God, I love this stuff."

"Nurse Rhodes. This is for my protection and yours. I advise all staff to take similar precautions in case the weapon has abilities we do not yet know." He tapped the table. "You did not see what was left of Doctor Hamilton."

Sherri shuddered. "Hard to believe that child is capable of such violence."

"That child revels in it." Doc Brown Eyes stood. "God help anyone who doesn't see her for the monster she is." He walked briskly out the door.

Rissa stared after him and felt her concentration waver. She pulled Sherri gently back to her bed, where she sat the entire time. Rissa gently eased her back to her pillow and covered her. Rissa vanished with a thought but stayed asleep at the facility.

She reveled in killing? Rissa fought through another bout of nausea and reached for one of her favorite memories. It wasn't exactly hers, of course, but she borrowed it from one of her targets.

The waterfall appeared before her. The sound of the rushing water music to her ears. Rissa sat on a rock close to the din and felt drops of water fall on and alongside her. The surrounding foliage green beyond any she'd seen before. Vines, trees, and tropical flowers bloomed and framed the spectacle. The smell earthy and humid. A gentle breeze blew, and Rissa lifted her face to capture it.

This was all she wanted. Solitude. Sunshine. Solace.

Rissa rarely let herself visit because the rest of her life soiled this pristine place. She soiled this pristine place. She glanced around one more time and woke up.

****

The kills came quicker now. Rissa supposed her abductor spread the word about their efficient killing system. She killed at least twice a week. The diversity still surprised her, though it shouldn't. Every ethnicity you could imagine coupled with ages from nineteen to ninety-two.

Nearly a third listened to her conditions and worked with her. The others died horrible deaths of their own making. One particular political jackass in his sixties swore he would do unspeakable things to Rissa, and she listened to approximately five seconds of that before she brought his worst nightmare to life.

You see, this particular fellow took whatever he wanted his entire existence. Money, drugs, women, and status. If something shiny came into his sights, he grabbed it with both hands, no matter the consequences. When his best friend's sister turned fifteen, he raped and killed her. Thus began a long history of bad behavior and cover ups. Rissa didn't have to dig far to find the darkest shadow in his mind. She brought forth the image of the girl, and let the old fucker's head do the rest. He died eight minutes later. *Too soon*, Rissa thought. He should have suffered more.

People were odd and eerie. Riss brought things from her targets' shadows that defied logic and definition. Giant spiders. Snakes with two heads. Aliens. Massive sharks. Dinosaurs. Creatures with needles for teeth and buttons for eyes. Things that lived, and usually stayed, in mind shadows. But Rissa invited them out to play.

Everyone was afraid of something.

Rissa worked on the lab staff between her killing schedule. She wasn't sure which would be harder, Doctor Bennett or the guards? The medic was her last person to manipulate. Rissa needed Bennett on board, but he was Doc Brown Eyes' sycophant. Could she somehow work Nurse Sherri to give her a break somehow? Or would that put the nurse in danger?

She played a cat and mouse game with Doc Brown Eyes, and he knew all the holes and traps. How far ahead had he thought? Was there an end game? Would he some day simply put a bullet in her head and close shop?

Rissa was a serial killer, but she was also still a kid. If she were not within these four walls, she could have everything she wanted. Someplace to call home. Groceries she chose. Clothes she picked. Patience, she reminded herself. *Don't rush this.*

****

Rissa opened her eyes and took her bearings. Her back against a wall while she sat on a small bed. A male's bed. Said male wasn't in bed, though he should have been. A narrow aisle between the bed and dresser on one side and a techie's wet dream on the other.

She studied the lanky male. Caramel skin. Buzzed hair with a lightning bolt shaved in the left side by his ear. A planetary set of pajamas in light blue at least a size too small. Hands that flew over a keyboard and eyes that moved as fast over two monitors. He may as well have had GENIUS tattooed on his generous forehead.

"Victim!" Rissa raised her voice to gain his attention.

The asshole didn't flinch.

"Fatality number one!"

The young man paused and turned to his left to look at Rissa. His dark green eyes serious and intent. "Hush. I'm in the middle of something incredibly important." He put his finger to his lips, turned back around, and stroked all the keys.

Rissa did not care for being ignored, especially by a target. She slid from the bed and walked over to his computer cocoon. She searched for the damn cord, but there were a million of them. Screw that. She placed her hand on top of something, and the whole system died.

"Shit!" The young man tapped a few keys and glared up at her. "Really? That's how you do things? You better hope I didn't lose any of my research."

She sat on the desk beside him. "I'm here to kill you. Zero fucks for your research. That's the least of your problems. You probably hopped, skipped, and jumped into something your large but wee brain didn't quite comprehend and shared it with someone both interested but scared shitless. Now. You're supposed to die oh-so-not-suspiciously, and all your brain material will be harvested by others. Lots of brain smarts, but tiny street smarts." Rissa held her thumb and pointer half an inch apart.

"I'm having a nightmare," he muttered.

She shrugged. "You could say." Rissa frowned. "You're Kase, right?"

He nodded.

"And you're sixteen?"

"In a couple of months."

Rissa screeched so loud, Kase wobbled and nearly fell out of his chair. She slid from the desk. "I knew those fuckers lied to me." She turned back to him. "I don't kill kids. I don't kill anyone under sixteen."

"Okay?" His eyes darted around the room.

"Kase." Rissa put her hands together. "You have an amazing brain. Can we put it to good use, please? I need you to work with me, okay?"

He nodded.

"I'm not going to kill you. This causes a problem for both of us." Rissa sighed. "I will have failed my job which will result in beatings, starvation, and a whole lot of shit for me. I'll deal with it." She pointed. "You are the bigger issue here."

"You're serious. You're here to kill me. In my dream. What are you, twelve?" Kase studied her for the first time.

"I'm fourteen, asshole, and I can make this entire scene change in a heartbeat." Rissa arched an eyebrow. "What are you afraid of Kase?" She searched his eyes until she found it. "Oh, that's an odd one, isn't it?" Rissa opened her mouth.

"I believe you!" Sweat rolled down Kase's face. "Please, don't! I felt you, and your eyes changed color."

"Should have changed to yours." Rissa dialed down the terror. "If I don't kill you, someone else will. They'll keep coming until your research is theirs, and you're nothing but dust."

"More like you?" Kase couldn't hide his fear.

"There are none like me. Good thing for you." Rissa shook her head. "They'll make it look like you harmed yourself, or outright kill you." She touched the computer. "What did you do?"

He shrugged. "May have stumbled across a light source stronger than LED, lasts longer, and is cheaper. Cool little prototype I threw together." Kase grinned with pride.

"Oh." She threw up her hands. "Is that all? I mean, I'm sure the energy overlords on this planet are overjoyed." Rissa lowered her hands even with Kase. "Are you fucking serious?"

He nodded.

"Are you beginning to understand the shitshow you're headlining right now?" Rissa demanded.

He nodded again.

"Oh, my fuck." Rissa blew out a breath. "I only have experience with killing, I don't do the saving thing." She paced the small aisle in the bedroom. "You have to disappear. Literally. For good. No contact. No family." Rissa stopped by his chair and stared at him hard enough to make him flinch. "Are you even capable of that? Leaving everything? Because these people may hurt your family, too. Collateral damage, and they don't give a shit. You would be on your own, Kase. At fifteen. Book smarts. No street smarts. On the street. You might be giving up an easy death now for a hard death later."

"Is that your sales pitch?" he muttered. "Fuck." Kase rubbed his forehead.

Rissa let him have three minutes before she interrupted. "I'm running out of time. You tell me now."

"How did you find me?"

She frowned. "What?"

Kase looked up at her. "Did they give you a piece of my clothing like a tracking dog? How did you show up in my dream? How did you find me?"

"They usually give me something to follow." Risa paused. "But then I followed the gold string." She frowned. "A gold string. In your brain." Rissa stared. "You have something none of the others have. Why?"

"I'm not sure, but I think I felt when you tugged it." Kase tried to remember. "Only I was in the middle of an equation, and I couldn't do both at once." He blinked. "Maybe you can still track me without the physical item."

"No." Rissa shot him down. "And I won't. I can block them from seeing what I do when I dream walk, but they watch my eyes. The fuckers can follow my mission through the colors. One slip, and I could endanger you." She felt an itch and knew she had little time left. "One day, I may escape, or I may rot. But I need you to be safe. Take your genius brain and build on it. Make your legacy large enough for others to stand on."

Tears slid down Kace's cheek. "I will." He looked up at her. "Your name?"

"Rissa." She disappeared.

CHAPTER 10

"Mission accomplished?"

The words rankled Rissa every time they brought her back out of her drugged sleep. She was more tired at the end of this so-called mission than the beginning. This was going to be a bad day. Still strapped down, she looked up at the lights on the ceiling.

"No."

Silence fell in Hell Hall.

The backhand to her left cheek stung, and she righted her head once again.

"Why?"

"I don't kill children."

Another backhand slap. Same cheek.

"You will terminate the target no matter the parameters."

Rissa clenched her jaw and prepared for the worst. "You'll go fuck yourself if it's a child."

Blinding pain in her face, and she passed out.

****

Rissa's face throbbed, and she kept her eyes closed. One of the medics placed an ice pack on the left side of her face, but it was now room temperature. She was sure one of these days they would break her nose. It seemed inevitable. She gently touched it and winced. Not broke. But certainly not happy.

"I don't like using your face as a punching bag."

"Yet you do it so well." *Oh, fuck.* Even her lips hurt.

"You are a weapon. We point you, and you discharge. What happened?" Doc Brown Eyes demanded.

"I told you what happened. I don't kill children."

"The target is gone." Dead silence. "Now. Tell me what happened."

Rissa sat up and threw off the defunct ice pack. She pushed herself up in bed and hoped she looked like she felt. The entire left side of her face swollen and aching. She couldn't open her left eye but stared at the brown-eyed remorseless fucker with her right.

"Funny thing. I landed on the target's bed. He was doing some next-level shit on his computer." Rissa leaned back against the wall. "I started to say something, and he hushed me. I proceeded to get his attention because I wanted to make sure this was my target, and I happened to ask his age." She touched the left side of her face. "He's fifteen. Out of my purview. I told him I didn't kill kids. Asshole was way smarter than me. He must have figured it out."

"Our client is angry."

"Did you tell him you slapped the weapon around so he feels better? Made her pay for having a rule she won't break. Make him feel better about himself? Surely that violence built a bridge between you. Did you sing a duet?"

Doc Brown Eyes snarled. "I explained occasionally our weapon misfires, but we will make amends. The client has given us two targets. We will eliminate them both for the pay he gave us for the last target."

"Will we?" Rissa nodded. "That's so good of us. I mean, I'd hire us. Hell. We're solid people."

"You'll prepare yourself for tonight. Two targets. You will not fail." The doctor stood up. "No pain meds until this mission is complete. Also, no food. We need you laser-focused on the removals. You'll never be a scalpel, but I won't stand for a sloppy machete." He turned and left the room.

Damn him to hell. Rissa blew out a slow breath on the good side of her mouth. Would she do it again? Yeah. She fucking would. She hoped boy genius ran like the wind, and these pieces of shit never found him. By this time, they'd have all his research. They simply wouldn't have the child to squeeze everything from. Not like her. The human sponge.

They never went two nights in a row nor did they point two targets. She eased from the side of the bed with a small curse and a big groan. Rissa shuffled into the bathroom. She used a wash cloth to dab at her face and clean some of the blood from it. Her stomach growled, and she bared her teeth.

Rissa dealt death. It was her companion. She didn't scatter happiness in her dreams like confetti, she dished last breaths filled with fear, terror, or shock. Everyone thought they would live forever. No one thought they would die in a dream. Yet, many did. She made sure of it.

Except Rissa.

Rissa tried it all. Slit her wrists. Shot herself in the head. Pills. Jumped off a roof. In front of a car. Knife fight. Toaster in her bath. Drowning. Hanging.

Nothing worked. She couldn't die in her dream. As disappointments go, it was a big one. It was a puzzle she worked in her head over and over again. The why of it. When she solved that, she could finally be done.

They gave her zilch in her room to help a suicidal weapon out. She thought about trying to choke on the bath cloth, but she was too weak. It would disappear when they rolled her back this evening.

Fuck them, she thought wearily.

Rissa collapsed back on her bed and pulled the sheet over her shoulder. She was cold, tired, and sore. She said a little prayer everyone would die, especially her, and fell asleep.

****

Another unanswered prayer as a sharp object prodded Rissa awake as night descended. No matter where she was, she knew the night. Her face throbbed worse, but she made no sound as two guards escorted her down the long bleak hallway to Hell Hall. Rissa often wondered if death row inmates felt like this. But they, at least, found release at the end. She would wear a path in the tile walking back and forth to cause someone else's death. Cheery thought.

They never touched Rissa as they flanked her. No need. Where the hell would she go? There was only the big hall running by her door and two doors, one on either side, as she approached her destination. Everything locked and secured. If they were caught in her dream? Their insides would splatter the walls like so much wallpaper. But Doc Brown Eyes made sure that never happened.

All six guards were fit and trained in military combat. One underweight teenager girl? They could, and would, snap her like a twig. She feared they would put her in a coma and somehow still use her abilities. She couldn't allow that to happen.

They took their job seriously after the doc spread a rumor about one guard who forgot his visor. Rissa supposedly saw his eyes, entered his dream, and slit his throat for payback. That's one way to make sure your employees wear their hazard gear. It also made sure they looked at her like the dangerous weapon she was.

Six main medical personnel rotated to use and abuse her. The voice overhead never left whatever safe room he used. He had three nurses. Doc Brown Eyes, Bennett, and a female nurse stayed in the room while Rissa worked. The two guards also stayed. Not ideal conditions for a prison break. Not ideal conditions for anything.

Oh. Wait. For murder. Ideal conditions for dreamy murder.

Rissa didn't even glance at the doctors as she entered the room. She strolled to the hospital bed and hopped up like her pain level wasn't an eight, and she felt faint from lack of food. Rissa hoped she died on this godforsaken table tonight.

The guards strapped her in without saying a word and retreated to their wall.

She waited.

The overhead mic turned on. "For fuck's sake!" Then off.

Rissa heard shuffling and looked up to see a granola bar shoved in her face. "Eat this."

She blinked and stared up at the masked doctor who usually stayed in his safe place. "Is it chewy or crunchy? I can't do crunchy right now."

"Get back in your safe space, you chickenshit." Doc Brown Eyes was pissed. He jogged over and tried to snatch the bar from the doctor's hand. "She doesn't deserve anything until she finishes this mission."

"She deserves to eat, you sadist." Safe Space Doc broke off a piece of granola and put it in Rissa's mouth.

Honey something. Rissa's mouth watered as she chewed the tasty morsel. She would let Safe Space Doc feed her the entire thing. But what truly fed her right now was the interaction between the two. Information, so scarce to her, kept her alive here. They had no idea their exchange was better than a three-course meal.

"I handle the weapon. You record the data." Doc Brown Eyes pointed back to the door behind them.

"This is how you handle the weapon? Beat and starve her?"

"The weapon is none of your concern. Take your ass back to the lab and record data. That's why I hired you. If that's too much, you can leave. But you know the conditions."

Doc Brown Eye's words hung in the air.

"I'm aware of your conditions." Safe Space Doc bit out. "She will eat the rest of this granola before her mission and be well fed before any more of them. Lack of food will skew the data, and I don't like errors in my reports."

Rissa stared at the ceiling. She obediently opened her mouth for another piece of granola and chewed quietly as possible. She thought Doc Brown Eyes held all the power here. Safe Space Doc blew that perception out of the water. This was better than Christmas.

Doc Brown Eyes stomped back to the wall. Safe Space Doc fed her the rest of the granola.

Rissa swallowed the last bite. "Thank you," she murmured.

Safe Space Doc nodded and walked away.

They strapped her chin and pushed the IV.

Rissa knew it would be a bad one from the minute doc told her about it. This was payback, pure and simple. She didn't follow rules? She would have them shoved down her throat and up her ass. Doc was mad. The client was mad. Who would pay for that? The weapon, of course.

She appeared in a spacious bedroom, mid-day, in a high-rise apartment. It screamed "money" from the spacious closet to the gorgeous view to the expensive art hung on the walls. Silky clothes littered the bed with boxes strewn across it and the floor. Female, obviously. The target preferred pastels. Great taste.

"I'm so glad you're here!"

Girlish voices filtered through before two young blondes entered the bedroom. They wore cotton sundresses in peach and aqua. Wide-brim hats over youthful faces and sandals to match. Slim and athletic. They were young, beautiful, and about to die.

They were also twins.

Rissa's gut clenched.

"I thought we could grab brunch first. I know the cutest little café down on third." The blonde nearest Rissa motioned, and the other one nodded and then frowned when she saw Rissa.

"Your friend?"

Both blonde heads turned.

"I'm not her friend. Or yours." Rissa walked over and sat on the edge of the bed. "You're dreaming right now. Both of you." Her pale green eyes looked at one and then the other. "Seventeen. Full of life. Excited to meet each other here since you've both been at different schools."

"Who are you?"

"I'm Rissa. You're Lacey and Stacey. Seventeen. Only children of Bob and Mary. Lacey is going to be an architect, and Stacey is going to be a fashion designer. But…you aren't." Rissa shook her head. "I'm sorry."

"What do you mean?" Stacey walked over. "We're not?"

"Lacey knows."

Stacey stared at her twin. "What do you know?"

"She's going to kill us." Lacey stated the fact with no inflection.

"What?" Stacey moved backwards to put space between her and Rissa. "This is crazy. There is no way this is happening. What are you talking about?"

"I had this bad feeling for the past couple of days, but I couldn't pin it down. You know how I get them." Lacey looked at Rissa. "Why us? Why kill us?"

"I don't know. I'm only given the targets. No explanation."

"But both of us, correct?" Lacey glanced at her sister.

"Yes."

Lacey grabbed Stacey's hand. "We don't have a choice, Stace. We don't have any more time."

"This will kill Mom and Dad." Tears streaked down Stacey's face. "Lace, I'm not ready to die."

Lacey wiped Stacey's cheeks. "Neither am I, sis, but it's time." She held her sister's hand.

Rissa looked at the pair. This hurt in new and horrible ways.

"Can you make it painless?" Tears slipped from Lacey's eyes onto their joined hands.

"Of course." Rissa walked over and stood behind them. It was weak of her, but she didn't want to see their faces when they passed. She raised her arms and pressed her fingers to their temples. They crumpled to the floor like paper dolls. Rissa looked at their bodies, still joined at the hands. She buried the pain deep and marked it with Doc Brown Eyes name. It would be the first of many.

CHAPTER 11

They brought her out quickly.

Doc Brown Eyes hovered over her. "Mission accomplished?"

She glared up at him. "Yes."

He checked something on his clipboard and turned to walk away.

"I'm going to kill you." The words left Rissa's mouth before she gave them any thought, but she realized they were the truth.

Doc stopped and turned back to her. "You'll never leave this building, Red. Never breathe fresh air. Never feel the sunshine on your face again. There will never come a day you kill me. But whatever makes you feel better."

"Not a day, doc." Rissa stared at him. "A night. A night like any other when you fall asleep expecting sweet dreams, and I'll be there. Then you'll know. Know what it feels like to be a target. And you won't be able to do anything about it." She smiled.

Silence.

Doc Brown Eyes jerked his head toward the guards. "Take her back."

The nurse hurried over and unhooked her before the guards escorted her back to her room.

Rissa walked straight to her bed and lay down. She felt guilt because of the dream buzz, nauseous from lack of food, and pain because the left side of her face met Doc Brown Eyes' hand too many times.

A guard opened her door and wheeled in a tray. He stopped at her bed, removed the lid, and stepped back a couple of feet.

She made herself sit up. Rissa wonder if cook felt sorry for her. They made two pork chops with gravy, mashed potatoes, two rolls with butter, and a piece of apple pie. There was a large cup of ice water on the right side with two white pills, one large and one small.

Rissa dug into the food and ate everything but half the pie. It was sweet, and her palate wasn't used to it. She gratefully took the white pills and hoped to hell at least one of them was for pain. When she finished, the guard put the lid back on and stood there. She glanced up at him.

"You know you're not supposed to talk to the weapon. I can fire bullets out of my eyes and grenades out of my ass." Rissa yawned and motioned him and the tray away from her.

He moved slowly to grab the tray. "You kill people?"

She studied at him. "It's not my favorite thing, but yes. It's why I have these deluxe accommodations, and I look like a fucking junkie." Rissa moved her arms so he could see the inside of both of them.

"They should put you down like a dog, not feed you like a guest." The guard wheeled the tray out without looking back.

The door closed with a click, and Rissa stared at it.

Then she laughed so hard she fell back against the wall. One guard wanted to fuck her. One guard wanted to kill her. Rissa wanted badly to poll the other four.

She knew Doc Brown Eyes needed to hire guards who were a bit crooked. Straight and narrow didn't strap a woman to a bed and confine her to a room. It was a bit hinky. Shifty fucks.

Rissa patted her stomach and lay back in bed. Most people closed their eyes when they wanted to rest or relax. It was a roll of the dice, depending on her mental state. Maybe it would be kittens, and maybe it would be her slitting the throat of a sitting senator.

One could never tell.

Rissa tried to block all her "missions", but it only gave her a migraine. Wasn't it bad enough to be there the first time? Why did she have to relive it? Rissa became immune to most of the violence. How could she not? When it all became too much, she turned the scene animated. She stumbled onto the trick when a client paid her handlers to murder his wife.

The sweet brunette wouldn't harm an insect in the house. She was the most big-hearted person Rissa had ever been exposed to. This woman, *Annie*, Rissa reminded herself with a considerable pang of remorse, offered her lemonade in the dream. When it came time for Rissa to kill her, Annie patted her hand and told her she didn't blame her at all. Who did shit like that? Rissa strained her brain to think of a way to finish the mission and not see Annie, dead, in her dreams for an eternity.

The mission fucked Rissa up for days. She wanted to kill the husband, her handlers, and anyone else that touched this mission. Fuck all of them. They all deserved to roast and rot. She finally filed this indignation away with the rest. They probably thought she forgot. Rissa never forgot.

****

Three days later, a medic came in to check her hand. Rissa held it up and studied the medic trying to work around their gloves and suit.

"You could take your gloves off." Rissa smiled pleasantly.

The medic glanced up at her and shook their head.

"Yeah. That's what I thought." Rissa sighed and rolled her eyes. "Beware the serial killer." She wondered if it was the medic with the bracelet on. She'd been in too much pain before to pay attention to anything but that wrist.

The medic checked the burn and bandaged it loosely once more. The blisters shrunk, but she'd still burnt the shit out of both sides of her left hand. Fucking idiot.

Rissa watched the medic gather the supplies and decided to take a chance. She stared hard.

"Mandy," she whispered.

The medic's arm jerked, and she dropped the bandages before she snatched them back off the floor, shoved them in a pocket, and fled the room.

Rissa didn't even allow herself a small smile. She brought her hand to her face, winced, and set it back on her chest. Another piece of the puzzle. She'd been collecting them for years.

****

Rissa never thought about death. It was simply an end. If there were a price to pay for the lives she ended, it was her cross to bear. She didn't undervalue life and its possibilities, but she'd never been given the chance to explore either.

At the ripe age of fourteen, it invoked neither sadness nor sympathy. Rissa's capacity for caring left and never returned when she came across an older man who dreamed of raping his son. The cruelty this parent perpetrated on his child etched in Rissa's brain for an eternity.

She threw the man against the wall, away from the boy. Then she moved the rapist to the living room. Rissa felt pure rage for the first time, and she buried the target in it. The man held a deep childhood fear of spiders because he stepped on an egg sac once, and they came spilling out all over his shoe.

Rissa splayed the man out naked in the middle of the living room and let the party begin. Spiders of every shape and size poured through the walls toward him. They advanced on him like wolves on a sheep, and he screamed as such. The scritch scratch of their spider feet, more like paws, amplified for the target. The clickety clack of mandibles as they surged upon him. Then some eight-legged genius started a web.

When the first spiders touched him, the man babbled incoherently and tried to kick. No such luck. Rissa sat on the couch and watched. The arachnids bit him on every inch of exposed flesh and scuttled into every orifice they found. The man died of a heart attack within ten minutes. He, of course, actually sat beside her on the couch with his mouth wide and eyes terrified.

It was the beginning of a callous year for Rissa.

She barged into dreams like the sleep slayer she was. Rissa pried out the deepest fear and let it bloom in all its fantastic horror in the minds of her targets. Asphyxiation, flagellation, and death by a rusty knife. Drowning, elevator cable break, and buried alive. Electric chair, gunshot, and hanging. Falling off a roof, bitten by rats, and some fellow who watched too many action movies tried to go one-on-one with the current cinema badass. He ended up with his nose shoved into his brain. It was a short scene. And cut.

Rissa also became incredibly clumsy. It started when she wasn't paying attention one day and actually tripped over a guard's shoe. She hadn't slept well, and her mind was everywhere, but on a needle and a dreamy death trip.

She went down, face first, and caught herself with her hands before she smashed into the tile. Rissa glanced to the right, before the guard pulled her up, and saw camo sneakers. She cut her gaze to the left and saw black and white sneakers. Interesting.

"Clumsy bitch." The right guard cursed. "I'm not carrying your ass."

Rissa looked at him. "Fuck. Off." She shook off his hand and kept walking.

"You're damn lucky this place has cameras, bitch." Ah, Chet. Predictable as always.

"Yeah, yeah." Rissa threw her right hand up in the air. "Or you would do horrible, horrible things to me." She glanced back. "Lose the shield." She allowed herself a grin. "Say it to my face."

The left guard snorted, and Chet told her to get her skinny ass in gear before they hit Hell Hall's main doors. Called her a bitch again for good measure. Rah rah.

Rissa pushed the doors open and walked over to the hospital bed. Her palms stung a little, but what pain was that compared to the death she was about to deal? She hopped on the bed and waited.

Silence.

"Can I get a bit of help over here or what?" Rissa sat up on her elbows and scanned the room.

"Stand down."

CHAPTER 12

Rissa frowned. "Me stand down?"

"The client changed their mind." Doc Brown Eyes tapped his clipboard. "Nothing like cancellation at the nth hour." He motioned to Rissa. "You seem unsteady on your feet."

"Could be I'm a fucking pin cushion? Underweight? Psychologically tortured? Tired of trying to sleep with the fucking light on? Have a headache? Mentally ill?" Rissa shrugged. "You tell me, doc."

"You need to tell me when you don't sleep well."

Rissa blinked. "Are you fucking kidding me right now?"

"I'm serious."

"Cool." Rissa held up two fingers. "Your weapon can't sleep with the damn light on, and she has a banging headache."

"We'll cut the light at night." Doc Brown Eyes made notes on his clipboard. "I'll advise cook to broaden their culinary offerings. You'll also take a few more vitamins. I don't like the way you stumbled earlier."

Rissa would give up years of her life to shove that clipboard up Doc Brown Eyes' ass sideways. The thought brought a wan smile to her face.

The fucker saw the smile and interpreted it wrong. "You're welcome." He motioned to the guards. "Escort the weapon back to her room, please." Doc Brown Eyes paused. "You may change your dinner routine, or take a rain check. Up to you." Then he turned on his heel and left the room.

"We could all have dinner together." Rissa brought her palms up, as if to thread their fingers together, and smiled.

"I'd rather drink bleach."

Rissa's smile broadened. "Even better."

The guards yanked her ass off the hospital bed none-too-gently and pushed her toward the door. "You're so rough! Geez. I'm simply a child, you know. Look at my little self. You both outweigh me by probably two hundred pounds."

They stepped into the hallway.

"We should clear the air." Rissa sighed. "Listen. That whole 'I killed the security guard' thing? Doc made that up to scare the shit out of you guys. Never happened. I didn't kill anyone on staff."

They walked toward her door.

"You never killed anyone on staff?" *Ah, Chet. So predictable.*

"Oh. Well. Staff at an earlier facility." Rissa nodded with her back to them. "Sure. Fucked him up so badly he looked like spaghetti when I was done." She turned at her door and smiled at the guards. "This is me. Sweet dreams." Rissa opened the door and closed it behind her.

The darkest part of her soul hoped to shit those two assholes had nightmares all night.

Rissa went to the bathroom, washed her hands, and sat on her bed. Her stomach growled, and she ignored it. The shoes. The shoes occupied her mind. Chet and his camo. Left guard and his black and whites. It was a key. She turned it over in her mind. They wore fresh booties over the shoes and tape over the ankles.

She jumped when the door opened, and a medic brought her tray beside her bed. Rissa thanked them and lifted the lid. She had no idea what in the holy fuck was on the large white plate.

Something grey floated in a sea of brown in her soup bowl. A large piece of meat, maybe, crusted with something and covered with green something else took up a large portion of the tray. There were baby potatoes. Score! And then there was a square of bread with so many seeds in it, Rissa thought she may need a beak to eat it. She gently poked the meat and realized it was fish. She touched the grey thing in the soup and realized it was a clam.

Rissa put the lid back on the tray and pushed it toward the medic. "No. Bring me bread and water. I can't eat this." She looked up. "Please. I'm not being difficult. I will throw up if I try." She pushed herself back against her wall and waited.

The medic didn't say a word but simply rolled the tray from the room. Rissa's stomach pitched. Maybe she should have simply eaten the potatoes. Everything else sickened her. She hated seafood. The smell. The taste. Fish sticks were okay, if they were covered in ketchup. But a big piece of fish with that stuff on it?

Rissa waited, but no more food. She sighed and lay down in bed. Guess Doc Brown Eyes subscribed to the "eat everything on your plate or starve" mantra. Her stomach growled. God, she hated him so much. And her fucking lights were still on. She closed her eyes.

The door opened a couple minutes later, and Rissa opened one eye. A medic rolled in another tray. Rissa sat up in bed and waited. The tray stopped in front of her. Rissa lifted the lid.

Peanut butter and strawberry jelly sandwich. A handful of plain potato chips. Three chocolate chip cookies.

Rissa looked up at the medic.

"Cook didn't make anything else, so they swapped dinners. They said they wouldn't make seafood, anymore."

Rissa sat the lid down and grabbed the sandwich. She took a huge bite and lay back with a stupid grin across her face. It was so sweet; it made her teeth ache, but she loved it. Rissa took another bite and shoved a potato chip in as well. Now sweet and salty. She would take this meal any day of the week.

She sat up, sandwich half-eaten in her left hand, and ate most of the chips. Then back to the sandwich. Rissa saved the cookies for last. She didn't know if she could eat all three, but she didn't want them to go to waste. When would this opportunity come again?

Rissa finished the sandwich and smacked her lips. She drank some water and grabbed the cookies. They smelled divine. She bit into one, and the crunch took her by surprise. Rissa closed her eyes and let the flavors explode on her tongue. Sleep would be a long while coming, but she didn't care. She shoved the rest of the first cookie in and held the other cookies, one in each hand.

"Are you going to eat those?"

Rissa opened her eyes and scowled. "I was attempting to have a moment here."

"I can't leave with food uneaten or not back on the tray."

"For fuck's sake." Rissa shoved one cookie in her mouth and glared at the medic. She chewed it quickly and shoved in the other. She held up her empty hands, flipped the medic off with both, crossed her arms and lay back against her pillow.

The medic took the empty tray and left.

"Fucking cow," Rissa mumbled around her cookie. "Not like I'm going to hoard food." She swallowed her cookie. "Facility full of assholes." She walked into the bathroom to wash her hands and drank from the sink. Her stomach full and happy with sugar. Rissa couldn't wait to dream. The lights went off as soon as she lay down.

****

For a young woman who could go anywhere, Rissa dreamed of quiet places. Her favorite space consisted of a spherical room painted in green mist with high walls and a scooped ceiling.

Natural light filtered through the floor to ceiling window on the north side and speckled her massive circular bed with flickering shapes.

Rissa made the bed soft, and it sank with her body weight as she flopped on top. She rolled over to her stomach and looked out the massive window. Trees. She loved the greenery. Maybe these trees didn't even exist in real life, but they did here, and she loved them.

Rissa didn't come here often because dream walking for herself took a toll on her. She didn't understand the mechanics and likely never would, but forays for herself usually left her groggy. The cookies, however, helped fuel this little jaunt. Rissa felt more relaxed than she'd been for longer than she cared to remember. Normal people felt like this all the time. How...odd.

She recalled her dinner and smiled. Doc would never let her have cookies on purpose. Rissa ate nutritional meals, took vitamins, and drank water. Yet, she stayed malnourished and underweight. It made no sense to her, but Doc didn't seem to have a problem with any of that. But gee, notify him if she had sleep problems? Seriously? SLEEP PROBLEMS? She wanted to rip his balls off and feed them to him.

Rissa rolled onto her back and calmed her breathing. That was not for here. Here was normal Rissa, whatever that meant. No death. Only life. Her life. Rissa clothed herself in a light pink silky gown and focused on merely being. In the moment. In this refuge in her mind. Part of her wanted to stay here forever. Rissa wondered if she could. Maybe checkout one day and not go back online.

It was a thought she had more and more recently. Rissa knew she had a powerful mind, but she never pushed it to its limits. What could she really do? Could she alter reality through her dreams? The thought intrigued her.

CHAPTER 13

It took Rissa over six months to finally access Chet's dreams. She came close once, but the arrogant shit caught the hole in his shoe booty in time. She had to wait another four months before she succeeded. Success tasted sweeter than even she imagined.

Rissa appeared in Chet's bedroom where he snored loudly on his small black bed. He slept in a pair of incredibly tight red briefs. Rissa immediately looked away and studied the room. Chet liked conflict, no surprises there. Magazines about wars and battles. Books depicting bloody scenes perpetrated decades before on his dresser and nightstand. One-track fucked-up mind.

Chet lived in a small house with only three more rooms. Rissa wandered around the small space and noted the kitchen showed no use. Apparently, our boy ate takeout or ate at the facility. The living room dim and drab, decked out in various shades of dark brown. The bathroom? Rissa walked in and studied all the containers on the counter. The asshole didn't give a shit about his home, but he didn't go cheap on skincare or body products.

Rissa declared him an egotistical asshole, threw some pants on his ugly ass, and woke him up.

"Uhhh." Chet stretched and yawned. He glanced at the clock. "Too early for this shit," he mumbled.

She gave him a Saturday, a day off. Rissa wanted to watch him throughout the day. She didn't want to put her feelings on Chet as truths, even though some were probably right. Asshole liked violence. Asshole liked himself. Actually, she was two for two.

Chet sat on the edge of his bed and yawned loudly. He rubbed his hand across his face and smoothed his dirty blonde hair back. When he stood up, Rissa took in every detail.

Six-foot. Little better than average build with strong arms. Shaggy dirty blonde hair. Trimmed moustache and blonde scruff. Deep set blue eyes. Pronounced jaw.

Rissa made him skip the shower and dress in jeans and a plain white t-shirt. Chet ordered breakfast on his phone. Rissa didn't understand any of it, but she let it play out. He ate in the bedroom while he watched TV. Asshole didn't care about crumbs in his bed or anything else that dropped from his mouth. She made a face and skipped ahead to early evening.

Chet sat down in front of his computer, and Rissa watched over his shoulder. He opened up some emails and then watched videos. They were violent videos of bombs, guns, and deaths. Rissa could see how excited Chet became the more he watched. This was his porn. Blue eyes glued to death and destruction. Ordered more food. Grittier videos. Hardcore military violence. He typed in another slew of words, and Rissa turned her head. Violence against women in specific and imaginative ways. She quickly withdrew from his dream and back to her own head where, though extremely murdery, it was safe from revolting scenarios Chet embraced. Sick fuck.

Rissa drew deep and steady breaths. Back in her own mind, she did a bit of housekeeping and filed what she knew about Chet away and attempted to ready herself for the morning. The next walk she did in his twisted mind would include a field trip to the facility and a day filled with bits of information she must file away for her escape. Careful, she thought. One small misstep could take her back to the beginning, and she couldn't afford that.

She had Sherri. She would have Chet. Chet would lead her to his partner, she hoped. Then Bennett. And the medic.

Rissa's numbers, one through five. She would make it out alive.

But honestly? She would kill herself before she came back to this cage.

****

Rissa followed Chet twice more at his house and three times to the lab. She finagled his partner's name on the last visit to the lab, when the dark-skinned Rajon, sporting stitch braids and full facial hair walked in at the same time.

Rajon seemed the opposite of Chet. Thirties. On the stout side, but solid. His voice low and soft. He came in, nodded, and found his locker.

Chet called over to him and asked about a poker game. Rajon simply shook his head.

"Hey man!" Chet's loud voice echoed against the lockers. "You're missing out. Going to have plenty of girls and booze."

Rajon shrugged. "I keep my own company."

Chet rolled his eyes. "Of course you do," he muttered. Chet slammed his locker and left.

****

Rissa left him immediately after that and woke, but stayed immobile, in her bed. Her mind picked apart the two guards, and she rooted around to figure out their role in her escape.

She hated Chet. Rissa would break out on his watch and burn him from his mind down. Doc Brown Eyes would be fucking furious, and Rissa tried to calm her pulse. They would soon bring her breakfast, and she needed to be nearly as catatonic as they wished she was.

Rissa needed to access the medic. She'd left an open door with the bracelet, and Rissa wasn't one to let an opportunity pass by.

But was it a trap? It could always be a trap. Better safe than tranquilized.

It was too soon to dream walk in another employee. Rissa truly needed rest. She would give herself two or three days to prepare and then stroll into the medic's head.

****

The day after, it was murder as usual. Some low-key foreign national aide. Blake something or other. Poor man fell of the hotel balcony from the fifth floor and splashed to the pavement below.

He'd been a hard bastard. Young but arrogant. Six-foot-four of fuck around and find out. He thought himself invincible and told Rissa as much. She wondered how the pavement tasted.

Rissa tried a free fall from a hotel balcony once. Landed on her fucking feet like a damn cat. Disappointing as shit. She dismissed the fleeting thought as she concentrated on her dream walk the next day.

She tried to relax and focus on the upcoming walk. Rissa ate her food like a good girl and took all the shitty vitamins they gave her. A brief shower and change of scrubs. She looked at the threadbare baby blue pants and noticed a string. Too afraid to pull it, Rissa sighed and lay back on her bed.

Soon, she promised herself. Soon she would wear clothes she picked. Eat food she wanted. Enjoy privacy, whatever that meant.

Rissa turned on her side and faced the wall. Oh, medic. You better not screw me over. Or it'll be the last time you have a chance.

She inhaled twice before she exhaled into Dream Land.

****

Rissa found the door immediately. Disappointed, she knew she left herself vulnerable when she opened the door. The only saving grace were the many glittery butterflies adorned from top to bottom on the plain oak entrance. However, a beautiful face could hide a multitude of sins.

She turned the knob slowly and braced herself. First sign of a problem? Rissa would tap-dance in the nurse's skull like kids given their first tap shoes.

Rissa didn't like dark rooms. They conjured up memories of pain and misery. Needles and nightmares. She kept the bathroom light on in her room when Doc agreed to turn off the overhead. When she stepped into a target's dream, she had all the power and control, and there was always a light on.

But not this time.

Rissa sensed the other presence but sat patiently in the dark and waited for her to speak.

"Thank you for this." The voice soft and modulated with the slightest southern accent. "I'm Barb."

"You're welcome." Rissa took a deep breath. "This is the only stipulation I can give you. Burn me, and I'll lobotomize you in the time it takes for your heart to beat. Understood?"

"Perfectly."

More silence.

"I don't enjoy seeing you strapped down and forced to use your skill for others. I don't like you're a prisoner for the gift you've been given."

Rissa forced a laugh. "You don't like a lot of things, yet I remain a prisoner in flesh and killer in mind."

"You know, as well as I, that if I were to make the slightest move to help you, they'd kill me. This is the best way for us to communicate."

"Why help me at all?" Rissa waited to weigh the next words carefully. She still wasn't convinced this wasn't a trap. Perhaps Doc Brown Eyes found another way around her defenses. Paranoia kept her alive.

The silence stretched out farther, but Rissa refused to break it.

A small sigh. "I have a daughter. She's mentally challenged. Mandy made me realize I can't leave you where you are."

"The bracelet."

"Yes."

"You feel guilt since you have a disabled female child? You're not sickened I plow through peoples' heads and basically blow brains out? Introduce them to their vilest nightmare or darkest thoughts and instigate total body shutdowns? Make their last moments their absolute worst?"

"You're a survivor, Rissa. I see the track marks on your arms. The hollowed-out cheeks. The frame of a twelve-year old." The voice softened. "But your eyes blaze, child. All your fire and spirit in those light green eyes. They scare the hell out of everyone, you know. But I love them."

"I scare people?" Rissa sat forward, greedy to know how she affected others.

"I've watched you go under half a dozen times." The medic paused. "The nurse presses her spine so hard against the back wall, I'm surprised her vertebrae doesn't fuse with it. Bennett walks as if he's navigating a mind field when he walks over and lifts one of your eyelids. He's scared shitless. His hands shake, but he tries to hide it. Boss shouts orders, as if he's running the show, but he never steps within twelve feet of you. The guards stay at the doors. If given a choice, they would exit the room, I've heard them talking, but Boss won't allow it." She chuckled. "When you go to work, the silence in the room is deafening. No one moves. I don't know if anyone breathes."

"More," demanded Rissa. Her blood rushed through her veins on a high she rarely experienced.

"Then you exhale the tiniest bit, and the room relaxes. The nurse unhooks you. Boss waits for you to come back. He asks his question. You answer. The guards come and take you away. Once the doors close, the medical team acts like they've had a brush with death, themselves. I don't think they even realize their actions."

"Tell me."

"Sherri immediately rips her helmet off and sucks in air like she's been deprived oxygen for hours. Bennett takes his entire suit off and leaves the room as if he's being chased by the devil. And Boss?" The medic paused. "He taps his clipboard rhythmically and repeatedly. I'm convinced he doesn't even know he does it. Then he disappears through the lab door to check results."

"I scare them." Rissa savored the words. She took a moment to picture everything and smiled in the dark. The smile faded. "Why are you working for them?"

Barb sighed. "Even after I picked up extra shifts, I didn't make enough to cover my bills and Mandy's expenses. I answered the ad in the newspaper for the facility. It seemed like a perfect job. I signed the non-disclosure agreement. That's when they reveal we are caring for a prisoner. A prisoner who can kill with her mind." She paused. "We're advised not to quit. If we'd like to transfer, it will be taken into consideration."

"You'll have a bullet in the back of your head, or I'll come visit you in a dream. Correct?" Rissa waited for an answer.

"Most likely." Barb shifted around. "There's a lot of money involved, Rissa. Some of the equipment they're using to track your brain signals and other variables is incredibly complex. One measures the oxygen in the room. When you go deep, oxygen rises in the room. You rarely use any at all. Sometimes I wonder how you're even breathing."

"This is what I need to know!" Rissa blew out a breath. "I need your help with all of this."

Silence.

"I won't risk my daughter for anyone or anything." Barb's voice strong and sure.

"No. I won't ever risk another child." Rissa swore. "Slow and steady. I already have a plan in place."

CHAPTER 14

There were three days without dream walks. Barb explained to Rissa that Boss planned a marathon murder the third night.

While that sounded super fun, Rissa gathered her strength and planned her escape. On the third morning, she set her scheme in motion.

Chet liked to roam the halls as he became twitchy if he sat too long. Not enough violence porn and brutality to satisfy him. His partner, Rajon, stayed in the security room with all the cameras.

Rissa planted toggles in Sherri, Tommy, Chet, Rajon, and Barb. She hated to do it to Barb, but the nurse understood and agreed immediately.

Doc Brown Eyes calculated prep time and gave himself permission to arrive an hour later since he stayed up deep into the night for a last-minute addition to the assassination.

Three targets acquired. Rissa needed to make one of the targets shoot the other two. It would demand a great deal of energy, and Doc Brown Eyes wanted to ask cook to prepare special food and drink. They would begin early and work late into the night.

If Rissa succeeded, Doc Brown Eyes would add another skill into her portfolio and increase her value. If she didn't, well, he would have to *persuade* her to try again.

Rissa knew bits and pieces of Doc Brown Eyes' plan. What he didn't know is that she could already plant triggers and toggle people into a somewhat fugue state. Perfectly functional but slightly hazy on the details.

It took Rissa years to come to this point. Years of abuse and torture. Years of murder. She combed every minute detail until she could run the plan forwards and backwards. In her mind. Relying on others did nothing for her confidence, but there was no other way. And in the spirit of karma, it was literally the least they could all do.

She only needed to make her way from her room to the other side of the lab and into the kitchen. Nothing but woods greeted her from there. The parking lot lay right outside her bedroom wall, and that was but another risk she would have to take.

Timing.

Everything was timing.

Rissa intended to escape in seven minutes. Then the staff's toggle would reset back to normal.

She lay in her bed. Heart beat racing. She strained to hear something. Anything.

Two light taps on her door and the mechanical sound of someone using their key card.

Rissa jumped up from her bed and eased the door open. Chet walked down the hall toward the security room. His heavy steps echoed in the hall, and Rissa counted to thirty.

She opened the door, only enough to squeeze through, and crept into the staff bathroom next to her room. Sherri thoughtfully placed sweats, a hoodie, and shoes folded on the toilet. A knife shone on top in the fluorescents.

Rissa threw off her scrubs and slipped into the oversized clothes. She palmed the knife and hoped she wouldn't have to use it. And let's be honest, it wouldn't be on staff.

The shoes felt like heaven, and Rissa inhaled the fresh scent of leather. Her bare feet long used to traipsing up and down the cold tile from bed to lab and back again.

She didn't waste a second.

Chet and Rajon "watched" the security cameras, but they were the ones offline. They killed the alarm, and Rissa felt the incessant hum die immediately.

Sherri needed to return to the lab and prepare for the day's proceedings.

Rissa stepped into the hallway when she heard a scream. Her head whiplashed to the sound, and she fought not to join it.

Had to be Sherri.

Rissa didn't build in blinders for Sherri because the nurse wouldn't need them. Short drop off and back to the lab. Something happened that broke Rissa's toggle on her, and that was not in the plan.

"Spider!" Another shriek. "Someone needs to come and kill this spider. We're a fucking lab, for fuck's sake! How the hell did it get in?"

Rissa frowned at her words. She put a light toggle in the nurse and medics because it was simpler. Apparently fear switched that shit off like a finger snap.

Fuck.

Rissa ran to the room across from the bathroom and shut the door quietly. Time ticked on. Her time. Her life. She turned around and blinked.

Filing cabinets on every wall. Information. Her information. Rissa silently counted in her head and then took a risk. She grabbed the nearest filing cabinet and opened the top drawer. Notes from two years ago.

Subject behavior shows an increase in defiance. The weapon continues to stretch out the time in the dream walk. Will enact a correction to rehabilitate.

A week later, and the weapon now understands they

are inconsequential except for the assassination. Medium-high correction procedures needed.

Rissa pulled the entire file out and shoved in the back of her sweats. There was no way she could afford to wait and search through more files, but she wanted something to take with her.

"I swear to God! If I see that spider again, I'm filing a complaint with the boss."

Sherri's mutterings strong and clear through Rissa's door. The nurse locked herself into the staff bathroom. Rissa's hands shook as she fled one room for another.

The door slid quietly closed, and Rissa pushed the lock in with a sigh. Time ticked. And that bitch Sherri ate it like chocolate candies.

Machines whirred and beeped behind Rissa. The room reeked of metal. Her nose, sensitive to some odors, twitched. The sneeze built until Rissa ran to the farthest side of the room and buried her face in her hoodie.

The sneeze left Rissa weak and dizzy. No breakfast today, and she hadn't slept last night because of anxiety. She held her hand against the nearest wall and sniffed quietly.

The staff bathroom locked click once more, and Rissa stood stock-still. She couldn't have Sherri roaming the halls with her. One more fucking shriek, and the knife in Rissa's hand would only have one more use.

Rissa crept to the door and turned the knob slowly. She eased the door open and heard Sherri's shoes shuffle farther down the hall.

That was the bitch of it. The lab took up nearly the entire hallway. Safe Space Doc's lab and the security room shared a wall with it.

Rissa eyeballed the next door and hoped to hell she would make it. She froze immediately.

"Has anyone seen Tommy?" Sherri's shrill voice sounded closer. "He'd kill the freaking spider."

Shit, shit, shit. Of course, Sherri turned around. Tommy and Barb sat in the Medic Lounge exactly where Rissa put them. Exactly next door.

Rissa looked behind her at the server room and made an executive decision. She ran into the Medic's Lounge and hid in a closet.

Both Barb and Tommy not only looked at her, but they looked through her. Rissa hid in the closet, behind a flimsy chipboard door.

These assholes strapped her down to a steel bed, watched her with pricy security cameras, and tracked her "events" with the most expensive tech around. Way to go on the fucking door, though.

Sherri barged through a minute later and sighed. "There you are, Tommy. Didn't you hear me?"

"What?" Tommy lifted his head and smiled. "What didn't I hear?"

"There's a fucking spider in the hallway!" Sherri rubbed her hands up and down her arms. "I hate those things. Creepy-ass, eight-legged having assholes."

Tommy hid a grin. "They eat other bugs."

"Other bugs?" Sherri looked around. "Jesus. We have other bugs?"

"No. Because we have that spider." Tommy calmly took a sip of his soda and studied the nurse.

"Fuck you, Tommy. Come kill this son of a bitch before I report you for goofing off on the job." Sherri's eyes dared Tommy to say another word.

"Can I at least roll my eyes?"

Sherri growled. "Not if you want to keep them."

"Is there a reason you can't acquaint the arachnid with your size 9 shoe?" Barb held her hands up like a question.

"Size 7," Sherri corrected her with an icy glare.

"Tommy." Barb turned to her partner. "I realize you are certified to save lives, but today, today you must take one."

"Fuck both of you." Sherri's breath came hard and fast. "Ever had one of those motherfuckers down your shirt?" Her blue eyes sharpened in remembrance. "All eight legs scratching your skin. Looking for a way out. Fangs biting when it panics." She shuddered. "I needed medical treatment. Still have a scar on my back."

"Okay, okay." Tommy stood and pointed. "Lead me to the victim."

"About damn time," Sherri huffed and stormed out.

Rissa waited a beat after the door closed to step out. Another vague glance from Barb, and she went back to the newspaper. No phones allowed in the building.

Rissa opened the door and ran for the next. The clock ticked loudly in her ears, and she held onto the ticking with a desperation born of necessity.

Two minutes.

If she could only make it to the kitchen, Rissa stood a chance. And the cook, whoever it was, could either let her pass or meet the knife she clutched with white fingers.

Rissa ran to the locker room and wound her way to the pantry. Barb told her they shared a doorway so the guards could simply grab the food and transport it.

The smell hit Rissa first. Her stomach clenched and growled at the promise of food, and she grimaced. Some type of meat. Potatoes. Rolls.

Her mouth watered, and Rissa told herself to be strong, at least for the next minute and a half. That meal was supposed to give her strength for a multiple murder that evening. The thought sobered her.

Rissa shoved the door open with her left hand and stabbed with her right. She didn't know who was more surprised, her or the man frying potatoes on the stove.

He was a big man with dark brown skin and light brown eyes. He wore blue jeans and a black t-shirt that praised pork butt. The man wore heavy black gloves and scowled at her.

"What is your white ass doing in my kitchen with a knife?"

Rissa grabbed a roll from the sheet to her right and took a bite. She shoved as many as she could into her pockets. She chewed quickly. "Pretend you're scared of me, please. Or they'll kill you." She glanced up at the cameras and away.

He wasn't slow. The man turned the stove off and put both his hands up. "What's going on, girl? And look at me. Do I look like I would be scared of you?"

"You the cook?"

"Yes."

"Thank you." Rissa grabbed another roll. "Listen. I'm escaping. I need to get you out of the way, or they'll think you helped, and they really will kill you."

"I've been feeding you?" He looked at her slight frame and anger built like a storm cloud on his face. "I've been cooking, but they haven't been giving you my food, have they?"

"Long story." Rissa held up her hand with the knife. "Listen, I'm a killer. Biggest threat ever. I need to leave now."

"Refrigerator. Opens both ways." The man kept his hands up as Rissa walked him over. When they were out of camera range, he turned. "Otis. You are?"

"Rissa."

"Rissa. My jacket is on a hook on your way out of this building. You take that money, child. All of it. Don't have any cards 'cause I don't trust them." He looked her in the eye. "Now, you get the hell out of here, and don't look back."

She shut the door and stuffed another roll in her mouth as she threw open the door between her and freedom.

Bright.

Rissa threw up her hands to block the sun and blinked rapidly.

Trees. Now.

Rissa flipped the hoodie over her head and took off at a run. She praised the heaven on her feet and found shoes a wonder. Rissa knew she was weak and at every disadvantage that existed. But adrenaline kicked in, and she disappeared into the forest.

CHAPTER 15

Rissa ran away from the sun and hoped her built-in cushion for time didn't fail her. What would she have at the most? A couple hours? Good thing being that Doc Brown Eyes couldn't call out the National Guard without raised eyebrows. But guns for hire? Oh, yeah. Guaranteed.

The first night Rissa spent in the free world, she walked as far as she could in back alleys and overgrown areas. Bugs ate her up, and she didn't give two fucks. Being a pin cushion for a decade of one's life made her immune to the bites and pricks. When she couldn't walk, Rissa stopped in a copse of trees and climbed the one with the fullest branches. The moon rose, and she shimmied into a crevice more than half the way up. Her small frame eased back, fully ensconced, and Rissa slept.

She dream-walked out of necessity. Someone nearby kept dirty money. Odds were for it. Rissa reached for the nearest neighborhood and walked down the row. She hit pay dirt on the fourth house. Robbie embezzled money from his boss. Separate bank account. Five digits. Certainly nothing to sneeze at. He funneled it every pay day and would quit when he hit six figures. Rissa made the necessary adjustments and left the way she came. She eased back into sleep and waited.

Early the next morning, Robert Norris stopped at his bank and made a twenty-thousand-dollar withdrawal in mixed bills. He assured the bank there was no problem. He simply wanted to purchase an older car and pay cash. They filled a bag, wished him a good day, and he left. Robbie then hopped in his car, drove to a small field of trees two miles from his house, and placed the money about hundred feet in, at the base of one of the biggest trees. He smiled and whistled as he walked back to his car. Then he drove home, readied himself for work, and arrived a bit late.

Rissa watched Robbie leave the money, and she didn't waste a second. She knew the lab and its ilk needed to find and kill her. No more needles and hospital rooms. The weapon committed the foulest deed. She escaped.

Rissa knew the odds weren't in her favor. But she broke out. That was against the odds. Maybe she should stay in place another night. No. Bad idea. Keep moving. Keep moving. Rissa couldn't stay at any shelter. They probably looked there first. The bus lines. Maybe they weren't looking for her at all. She grimaced. *Yeah, right.*

She walked through the nice neighborhood and then another. Most residents were at work, and she couldn't be happier. Rissa wanted to be at least a two-hour drive away from the facility. She didn't know why two hours was so important to her, but it seemed to be the magic number. The sun beat down on her, but she kept her hoodie up and hoped she looked like any one of the many other teenagers she saw around.

Rissa walked eight hours that day, and her entire body felt like it wasn't her own. It didn't matter. She fueled herself with convenience store sandwiches and caffeine. Her body rejoiced in the rush but demanded she continue to sate the fizzy demon, or her legs suffered as dead weights. She walked until the sun sank into the sky and found another thick set of trees to vanish.

The backpack wore on her, but she handled it as though it weighed nothing. These physical things were minor inconveniences. Rissa lived. She fought her way out of hell. The sky above. The earth below. The fresh air in her lungs. She would carry a boulder, if need be.

Rissa climbed another tree and situated herself into a large crack in the branch. She tested her weight, and it held. She put the backpack behind her head and wrapped her arms around herself. Even the night, with its bugs and noises, felt like a gift. Rissa listened for strangers for hours, until the moon rose high in the sky. She finally let the crickets sing her to sleep.

****

"I never hurt you, girl." The words spoken quietly in the dim room.

Rissa studied the man sitting in his chair from the doorway. He was large with dark brown skin. His hair braided and hung to his collarbone. Rajon wore no shirt, only a pair of pajama pants in dark green with matching slippers. Rissa could see the right side of his face. He was clean-shaven with dark brown eyes and full lips now pulled tight. The room smelled of stale cigarettes and cheap beer, but it was spotless.

"You knew I would visit?" Rissa walked into the sparse living room/kitchen and sat on a chair closest to the front door.

"Aye." Rajon looked at her. "No one did right by you. When you escaped, and we were sent away, I knew you would come calling."

Rissa stood up from her chair and walked a few steps toward the man in his. "You mean to tell me that you've never hurt me?" She stared him in the eye.

"Not personally."

"Ah. Not *personally*. Just a job, right?" Rissa's eyes darkened. She lowered her voice. "And why did you take this godforsaken job, Rajon?"

"My Mom was sick. She passed away a year ago. Lung cancer."

Rissa sniffed the air. "Following her lead?"

"Started smoking when you escaped," he admitted. Rajon shifted in the chair.

"It's fascinating." Rissa moved two feet closer. "You're right. You never personally hurt me. I can read it in your mind. Never threw me anywhere. Never called me a bitch. Never left a bruise on me."

"No, ma'am." Rajon put his hands in his lap.

"But you also never helped me. Personally." Rissa stressed the word. "While I was brutally handled daily by a murdering sadist, you did your job. It's a lot to swallow."

"Please. Don't kill me." He offered his hands, palms up. "They would've killed me for helping you. I had no choice."

"There's a title to my biography for you. 'No Choice' the Story of Rissa Clay." Rissa bared her teeth. "I had enough of that every day, Rajon. While you were eating good food and making good money, I was treated like shit and murdering people I didn't know. The scales are nowhere near fucking even."

Rajon bowed his head. "I'm sorry," he mumbled. "I know."

Rissa frowned. "What? What did you say?"

He looked up at her with tears in his eyes. "I'm sorry. I was selfish."

"Holy fuck, Rajon. I've never seen a man truly cry." Rissa stared at him, perplexed. She reached over and touched the tears on both cheeks. Then she brought her finger to her tongue to taste them. *Salty*. Rissa blinked. They kept coming from both eyes.

Rajon wiped the tears and stared up at Rissa. "I'm ready."

Rissa looked down at him. She didn't feel pity, but she no longer felt the need to disembowel him. "You still need to be punished, Rajon, but I won't kill you." He opened his mouth, but Rissa shook her head. "Not a word, and do not thank me. You make this choice. I will take one eye, or I will take both legs. Choose."

The tears came freely. "My eye," he whispered.

"It shall be." Rissa leaned down. "When I disappear, you will never have cause to mention my name again. Ever. Understood?"

Rajon was in the middle of a nod when Rissa plucked his right eye out and left his dream. The big man woke screaming, with blood streaming down his face, and his enucleated right eye in his hand.

****

The car horn jolted Rissa out of a sound sleep, and she nearly screamed before she realized her precarious position. She lay there while her heartbeat pounded frantically in her chest. Another car horn, and she rolled on her side to peep out of her nest.

Two men jumped out of their cars and waved their arms as they approached each other. The rest of the cars went around at the stop signs. Rissa frowned. It seemed stupid. Then the first man punched the second man. The second man punched him back. The fight began. She watched for a few minutes until the police came and escorted the men and then called someone to take the cars. Rissa hugged her backpack to her chest. She couldn't be seen by anyone, but especially the police. Fear, cold and clammy, encased her. How long should she wait? Would neighbors still watch? When was it safe? She took a drink of her warm bottled water and glanced around. Her entire life built on chances.

A slight breeze picked up as Rissa hit the ground by the tree. She held her face to the wind for a minute before she flipped the hoodie back up. It was a nondescript grey, same shade as her backpack. Rissa wore baggy jeans and a grey t-shirt. She had a ballcap in her backpack in case she wanted to wear it instead.

Rissa cut across the field and slowed down slightly at the four-way stop. She crossed the street before the signs and started down a neighborhood block. It was neither fancy nor plain but a nice row of houses with flowers in front yards and wind chimes hanging above. Yards were well-kept but not manicured. A few houses needed a fresh coat of paint, but it seemed a pleasant neighborhood. An occasional dog bark broke the silence.

She wound her way down the third block when a voice called out. Rissa kept walking.

"Honey! HONEY!"

Rissa winced and looked in front of her. Not a soul in sight. The voice loud and persistent behind her. What happened to being invisible? Besides, she looked like she slept in trash. Smelled the same. Rissa turned with a polite smile and yelled back, "No thank you!" and turned back around.

"Honey! I have something for you!"

And before Rissa could make a get-away, a fluffy woman in her sixties puffed up beside her with two small brown bags. The breath whistled in and out of her circled lips.

"Oh, honey. Make an old woman run. Not my best look." She smiled at Rissa with light blue eyes and silver hair in a bun on her head. She had a round face and a round body encased in a flowery jumpsuit with large purple and orange flowers from shoulder to ankle. "Oh, you're so tiny." She frowned. "I knew I was meant to give you these." The woman shoved both brown bags at Rissa.

"What are you giving me?" Rissa frowned and tried to give them back.

"Listen, honey." The old woman's voice softened. "I don't know what you've been through, but when I'm called to do something, I stand on it. I was sitting in my kitchen, and I looked out the window. And you know what I saw? I saw you. Shoulders slumped. Carrying the weight of the world on your shoulders. Trying to get away from something as quick as you can."

Rissa's eyes cut to hers.

"In one bag is a peanut butter and jelly sandwich and some chips. It's what I used to make my daughter for lunch every day for school. She would eat peanut butter off the spoon, if I let her. There's also a candy bar, though I don't know your preference."

The old woman cleared her throat. "I lost her a long time ago, but I hope you enjoy it as much as she did." She pointed. "The other bag has thick socks, deodorant, a toothbrush, and toothpaste. No one should have to do without these things."

"Thank you," Rissa whispered.

"Oh, honey." The old woman sniffed and wiped her eyes. "This is as much for me as it is you." She paused and then put her hands on Rissa's shoulders. "I pray you heal, child. I pray that all wrongs are set right." She dropped her hands. "I don't suppose you'd let me take you anywhere?"

"No." Rissa shook her head. "Too dangerous." Her shoulders still felt weird from the old woman's touch.

"Then this is it, child." The old woman took a deep breath. Her blue eyes both sad and kind. "Be safe, honey. I'll keep you in my prayers." She turned slowly and shuffled back to the house she hurried from. The screen door still open and swaying slightly in the breeze. She turned and waved to Rissa before she went back inside.

Rissa picked up her pace and hit the next block, nearly at a jog. She slowed down when she was out of sight and pulled the sandwich from its zipped baggie. The first bite? Pure heaven. Rissa breathed through her nose as she inhaled the sandwich and dug in the bag for the chips. These chips with a cheese flavor, but not bad. She washed both down with warm water and shoved the trash in the nearest bin. The candy bar put in her backpack in case she needed more sugar fuel.

The highway sounded closer as she moved to the northeast. Rissa needed at least eight hours travel time. That put her at roughly twenty-three hours away from the facility. It was half what she needed. She would travel four days to reach her destination to see if it was safe. If Rissa couldn't stop, she would continue to travel and work out what she would do next.

CHAPTER 16

Rissa eyeballed the objective from her hiding spot in the trees. She camped as high as she could reach in a solid tree with smooth bark. The nest gave her privacy and freedom to observe.

She ate another granola bar and situated herself against her backpack. Two days. Rissa would watch for two days. If no alarms, like mercenaries or big white vans, approached, then she would make her way down to the goal.

If Rissa felt a hint of something wrong, she would continue her hike, farther up the woods and into the great unknown. Rather than the known abuse and total destruction of her soul.

****

Two days came and went. Rissa nearly talked herself into waiting a third. The risk. It weighed on Rissa's chest like an elephant with bronchitis. Each breath pushed down in the middle. She felt as though she could drown without water.

Rissa looked at the houses scattered across the acres. Some were built close to the woods while others chose to keep their residents near to the only paved road. Good neighbors didn't need fences while some family kept a gate around their entire home. It was an interesting conglomeration of lifestyles and licensures.

She spotted the buttery yellow house immediately. It hung back, in its own row, away from the rest. The big back yard posted up against the thick woods behind it. It was adorned with rose bushes along the front, of pink, yellow, and red hues. The porch, handicapped-accessible, with windchimes singing in the breeze. Three large trees, one at each end and one at the middle, decorated the front yard. They grew a bit taller than the roof of the house and stretched branches to reach each other. *Mandy's house.*

Rissa walked casually from the trees, along the back fence-line to the door right beyond it. Her heart beat hammered in her chest. Years of planning. Hours of walking. Came down to one turn of a door knob. If Barb betrayed her, she'd kill herself before any of them touched her again. She slowed her breathing and turned the knob.

The door clicked, and Rissa pushed it open slowly. No sound came from within. She hurried inside, closed the door behind her, locked the knob, and turned the deadbolt. Goosebumps broke out all over her body, and her breath wheezed in and out.

Rissa walked down the short hall and stopped. She dropped her backpack at her feet, took off her hoodie and let it fall on top. Barb's kitchen, to her left, made her mouth water. There were cookies in a large clear jar that Rissa opened and grabbed two of the biggest. She shoved one in her mouth and closed her eyes in pleasure. Sweet. Rissa didn't know what kind but didn't care. She walked over to the refrigerator and opened it.

So. Much. Food.

She shut the refrigerator and stepped back. Barb decorated the kitchen in green and red. Apples in various shapes and sizes everywhere. There was something in a big brown round pot on the cabinet. Rissa put her hand near it and then pulled back. Hot. She ate the other cookie and grabbed two more. Rissa pulled water from her backpack and walked into the living room.

Barb used blackout curtains but left two of the living room lights on. Rissa touched the soft brown couches and noticed her filthy hand. She walked back into the kitchen and turned the sink on to wash the grime. She dried her hands on a nearby towel and opened the cabinets. More food. Chips.

Rissa grabbed a bag of chips and sat down on the smaller couch. She kept her knife in her left hand while her right hand fed her body. Barb said she worked until four-thirty and would be home by five. Rissa hoped Barb came home alone.

****

The deadbolt slid heavily over as the key rotated. The knob to the front door turned, and Barb kept her body in the space between while she opened one door and shut the other quickly. Rissa tensed and prepared to slit her wrist if anyone else appeared or breached the house in any way. She kept herself deathly still as Barb turned and faced the room.

"Oh." The small broken word left Barb's mouth the same time she spied Rissa on the couch. She dropped both bags she carried, and her purse slid to the floor. "Rissa."

Rissa watched the tears stream down Barb's face with no emotion. Guilt? Relief? "Why are you crying?"

Barb sniffed and held her head up. She blew out a breath. "I'm glad you're here. That's the truth. But you look like hell, child. You have cuts and bruises all over your face and arms. You need a hot bath, maybe two." She moved a few steps closer. "I put a roast in the crockpot. Can I run bath water for you? Maybe wash your hair?"

Rissa put the empty chip bag on the brown table in front of her. She unfolded her legs and stood. "I'll take a shower. You can brush my hair later."

"Okay." Barb nodded. "You're no bigger than Mandy. The top drawer in her room has her nightclothes, mostly tops and bottoms. Please help yourself. I'll finish making dinner. Let me know if you need anything." She bit her lip, as if she wanted to say more, but turned to walk to the kitchen.

Rissa walked down another hallway toward the bedrooms. There were two separated by one large bathroom. She walked into Mandy's bedroom and didn't bother admiring the girly décor of pink, purple, and blue unicorns and fairies. The glittery ribbons streamed across the ceiling and over the canopy bed, but Rissa paid them no attention. She hurried over to the dresser and pulled out a light green top with matching bottoms and scurried away like hell was on her heels. The room made her itch.

She shut the bathroom door behind her and clutched the clothes to her chest as she rested her head on the door. Rissa tried to calm herself. *Freedom*. She fought for this. It was hers. She put the knife on the sink and didn't bother to look at herself in the mirror. Rissa surely looked like that demon Doc Brown Eyes always claimed her to be.

The shower came on hot, and Rissa turned it down a bit and stepped inside. She bit back a scream as the water hit the cuts and bites across her body. Tears slid down her face and mingled with the stream that washed away the filth. Rissa stayed in until the water ran clear and tried to finger-comb her matted hair. She finally gave up and stepped out on wobbly legs.

The sugar rush wore off, and the exhaustion of the last few days weighed on her. Rissa wrapped a towel around herself and sat on the toilet. She needed sleep. There hadn't been any onslaught of guards or a smug doc so she would trust Barb.

"Barb," Rissa said. She cleared her throat. Her head felt like it had cotton in it. "Barb!" A bit louder this time.

Barb knocked and then opened the bathroom door far enough to poke her head in. "What's wrong?" She took one glance and hurried in. "Oh, honey." She stopped. "Can I put my arm around you to help you walk?"

Rissa hated herself but nodded.

Barb put her left arm around Rissa and helped her stand up. Then she led her out to the brown couch she sat on earlier. Barb helped her sit and then sat on the other end. The waterworks began again.

Rissa glanced up with a wan smile. "Are you going to cry every time you see me?"

Barb pulled some tissue from a box on the brown table and tried to stop the tears, but she couldn't. "You're beat to hell and back with bruises and bites all over your body." She sniffed and blew her nose. "You've mosquito bites next to pinpricks where Sherri stuck needles in you." Barb's voice hardened. "I swear to God, I want to wrap you in bubble wrap and disembowel every motherfucker whoever harmed you."

Rissa blinked. "What's bubble wrap?"

"What's...?" Barb trailed off and then gave a watery laugh. "I'll tell you later, child. First, please let me doctor your cuts and bites. I don't want them to become infected. And while I'm slowly torturing you, you should be awake enough to eat some real food. Then you can nod off. I'll grab your pajamas."

Rissa watched her hurry to the bathroom and looked down at herself. The towel covered her to mid-thigh. It was true. Her arms and legs were a nightmare of cuts, bites, and bruises. She couldn't see an inch of unmarked skin.

Barb returned with her clothes and a handful of boxes and tubes she put on the table. She walked into the kitchen. "I'm going to make you a bowl. It'll be easier to hold. It's roast with potatoes. I hope it'll set well with you and fill you up. Going to bring you a couple of rolls and some ice water to go with."

Rissa heard half of it because she picked up the nearest tube and tried to make out what it was. All she could see was something about bug bites. Acceptable. She put it down and picked up another.

"Here, child." Barb set the small tray down. The bowl steamed next to the water and rolls.

Rissa grabbed a roll and took a bite. So good.

"Now." Barb took each item off the table and explained to Rissa the purpose. She also said they may sting as bad as the bite or cut, depending on how deep it was.

"I think we both know I've been through worse." Rissa took a drink and then grabbed the steaming bowl. She dipped the spoon and slid a piece of meat on. She blew on it and then took a bite. Rissa moaned and closed her eyes. "I will stay awake until I finish this."

Barb chuckled. "Okay, Rissa. Don't say I didn't warn you. We'll do legs so you can eat." She tapped Rissa's right leg, and Rissa lifted it toward her.

"Fuck," the word hissed out between Rissa's lips as Barb found the deep cut on her ankle she caught on a bramble two days ago. She noticed the blackberries but didn't realize they were attached to an evil prickly vine. Barb cleaned and taped a piece of gauze over it. She moved on.

Rissa ate her food while Barb thoroughly cleaned, disinfected, and bandaged the hell out of her. She lost track of the many stings as she had lost track of receiving them. The roast and potatoes sat warm in her belly with the rolls and two pills Barb gave her for pain.

Barb put the towel in the laundry as Rissa put her pajamas on.

"Do you want me to brush your hair?"

Rissa shook her head. "Not tonight. I can barely keep my eyes open. Tomorrow. I need the rest."

"You do." Barb smiled. "You can sleep in Mandy's room."

"No."

"Oh." Barb's eyes widened. "Okay. I'm sorry. I thought you'd prefer a bedroom to a couch."

"Thank you, but I'd rather sleep out here." Rissa motioned to the couch she sat on.

"I'll bring out blankets and a pillow."

Barb hurried away and returned with two dark blue blankets and a light blue pillow. "I hope these will work." She handed them to Rissa.

Rissa took the offering and set it beside her. She gave her tray to Barb and watched her clean the kitchen and tidy up. She turned off the kitchen light and walked back into the living room.

"I'm leaving the night light in the kitchen on since you don't know your way around. If you wake up before me, help yourself to anything you want." Barb paused, as if unsure what to say. She bit her lip. "I know this is a lot, Rissa, but I'm glad you're here and safe."

"Are you going to cry again?"

"I'm thinking about it, smartass."

Rissa smiled softly. "Thank you, Barb. And I'll ignore the sobbing coming from your bedroom."

"You do that." Barb rolled her eyes and disappeared down the hall.

Rissa moved the couch pillows and put them on the larger brown couch. She put her pillow down and then a blanket. She settled herself on top of it and let herself relax into the softness. The cuts and bites ached and itched as they attempted to heal. The smell of the roast lingered in the air, and she rested her hands on her full belly.

Barb...surprised her. But maybe all mothers acted like that. Rissa would never know. She vaguely remembered her own with a twisted wistfulness. They had the same color eyes, and they laughed together. But her mother left her in the hands of those who hurt her repeatedly. Rissa could never see Barb doing that. Perhaps it was because of Rissa's defect.

Rissa wanted to sleep, but part of her feared the night and an onslaught of guards bursting into Barb's house. She grabbed the knife she now kept within arm's reach and put it under her pillow. Rissa pulled the other cover over her and finally drifted off.

CHAPTER 17

Rissa woke the next morning to the sound of humming. At least she thought that was the noise. She felt stiff and itchy. She cracked open her eyelids and peered into the kitchen. Barb slid around the kitchen, in her pajamas, to her nameless tune and took out items from the fridge. It looked like eggs, milk, and two other packages.

"Are you always like this at six o'clock in the morning?" Rissa muttered.

"Oh, shit." Barb turned with a wince. "I'm sorry. I didn't mean to wake you up."

"You were humming." Rissa arched an eyebrow. "Or something close to it." She stretched. "I'm going to the bathroom." She shuffled into the bathroom and closed the door. One look in the mirror, and she could see why Barb would shed a tear.

Rissa could never, would never, be girly. That part of her life taken by needles, ruthless people, and murder. She wouldn't wear bows in her hair or frilly dresses. No make-up, purses, or high heels. In all honesty, she couldn't mourn something she'd never been exposed.

But...her face. She bore a large cut on her right eye, a gash on her forehead, and small cuts across the rest of her face. Her eyes too large in this nicked-up mess. Rissa touched her hair and grimaced. Matted all to hell. Fantastic. She walked over to the toilet and pulled her pajama pants down. Her face almost pristine compared to the roadmap from hell across both legs.

Rissa pressed the large bruise on left knee and right thigh. Oh, fuck. Yes. Couldn't remember where she'd received either, but they represented some type of fall. Bug bites everywhere. Rissa could see where Barb rubbed in the cream and tried not to itch. Then there were the deeper cuts covered in light bandages. *Wow.* At this point, she didn't even really need pajama pants, she was basically covered in gauze.

She flushed the toilet and washed her hands. Even they took a beating. Rissa remember bloodied fingers, cuts, and endless pain. But that was then. She'd keep her hands clean. Rissa flexed them a couple times and smiled.

Barb smiled from the kitchen as a couple somethings sizzled on the stove. "Eggs, bacon, and biscuits."

They smelled glorious. Rissa nodded and walked into the kitchen. "Can you show me how to use the ice?" Barb showed her, and Rissa filled her cup and sat back down.

"How're you feeling?"

"Like something you'd find run over on the highway."

"Roadkill." Barb supplied the word.

"Huh?" Rissa took a sip of water.

"Roadkill. The things that are run over on the highway."

"Yes, then. Roadkill." Rissa filed the word away. "That's exactly what I feel like." She watched Barb make two plates and turn the stove off. "I'm ready to inhale breakfast. I seem to be starving."

"No wonder." Barb brought two trays and gave Rissa hers. Her dirty blonde hair up in a loose ponytail on top her head. "I know you ate three meals and snacks there, but it didn't seem like you gained any weight." She pointed to the tray. "Three eggs, two biscuits, and bacon. There's more if you're still hungry."

Rissa sat back and put her tray on her lap and watched Barb do the same.

"Thank you. Again." Rissa popped a piece of bacon in her mouth and chewed slowly. Decadent.

"I'm glad I could help in any way." Barb smiled at her.

Rissa knew she needed to say something. "I'm only going to stay a few days, and then I need to leave." She watched Barb hesitate for a minute and then take a bite. "I can't tell you how much I appreciate how much you've done for me, but if I'm here, you and your daughter are in danger. I won't have it."

Barb chewed her bite slowly. "It's been nearly a week." She looked at Rissa. "What are your plans?"

"You don't want to know." Rissa took a bite of her eggs. "And in that vein, you may want to take Mandy and visit someplace else for a while. Situations for former employees of the facility are not going to be safe for the foreseeable future. I'm sure someone will check to see how you're faring. If you disappear, it's a good thing on two fronts."

"All of them?" Barb asked in a low voice.

"The lion and zookeeper don't have the same perspective, Barb." Rissa took a sip of water. "Not everyone used the whip, but there were plenty who did and enjoyed it. Then you have the ones who ran the place. Guess what? There are others. Other places that exploit children and their abilities. We both know they'd put a bullet in a baby's head before they'd let them leave."

"You're going to go marching through their heads and take them all out? You don't think they're prepared for you? They had you for ten years, Rissa! Ten fucking years! You are not a mystery to them." Barb threw up her hands. "Jesus Christ! Why do you have to walk back into the fucking fire?" Her blue eyes blazed with emotion.

Rissa looked at Barb with something close to affection. "You indignation is noted and appreciated." She paused. "I'm it, and we both know it. I don't have a family they can hurt. If I try and fail, that's it. No repercussions to anyone else. But if I succeed, I can save who knows how many."

"They'll expect you." Barb's mouth drew into a straight line.

"They'd be stupid, if they didn't." Rissa held up her empty plate. "More bacon?"

Barb stood and grabbed her plate. "And she wants more bacon because of course she does. Asshole," she muttered.

"That's me," Rissa yelled back. "Also, can you do something with my hair?"

****

Rissa may have not thought things through when she asked Barb to brush her hair. The older woman enjoyed herself far too much, and Rissa far too little. She hadn't realized how many knots and tangles she had nor how fine her hair. She sat between Barb's legs on the floor while Barb sat on the couch and pulled her hair out.

"For fuck's sake, Barb! Leave a little on top!" Rissa clenched her teeth as Barb raked the brush through her hair again.

"Child. This is a detangling brush. It's trying to do its job. When was the last time you brushed your hair?"

"The lab's hair and make-up department left a lot to be desired." Rissa crossed her arms and didn't say another word.

"That's what I thought." Barb held down the hair closest to the scalp and brought the brush down through the snarled ends with a satisfied smile. "You really do have gorgeous hair, not that you care a bit."

"Do you do this shit to Mandy?" Rissa demanded.

"Yes." Barb patted Rissa's shoulder. "And she loves it. Once we get past this first tangled part, I think you would love it, too."

"Once you're done brushing, we're putting it up and leaving it the fuck alone." Rissa held both thumbs up and went back to the thoughts in her cluttered mind. Three more days at the most.

Barb would follow her schedule as if she didn't have a houseguest. Rissa reached out and had a little fake identification made and sent to Barb's house. The picture had a tiny smudge on it, but that was the point. Every bit of information on it, fake as the smile Rissa would give when she rented a cabin up the road. A little over an hour walk by foot.

Cain's Cabins offered one and two-bedroom cabins for the thrifty consumer. Not a lot of amenities as far as that went, but Rissa didn't need frills. The cabins weren't stacked on top of each other, and that was another perk. The gravel road wound through the forest of bushes and trees progress failed to damage yet. Thirty acres with ten cabins. Rissa looked everything up on Barb's computer, with Barb's help, and made her plans.

Barb took one final swipe through Rissa's hair and smiled. "I'm through. Let me see."

Rissa pasted a smile on her face and turned around.

Barb's smile faded. "You're so young. You remind me of Mandy." She put her hand underneath Rissa's chin. "I know you don't give two shits, but you are beautiful, Rissa. I wonder if you take after your mother."

Rissa shook her head, and Barb's hand fell. "Doesn't matter. Now." She motioned to her head. "What are we doing? Cutting it? What?"

"We can, if you like." Barb picked up the side. "It's halfway down your back now. We can bring it up to your shoulders or higher. We can also braid it or simply put it in ponytails."

"Cut it." Rissa looked at the length and frowned. "It's a handicap. Easy to grab. I don't want it." She looked at the time. "Can I make a sandwich?"

Barb nodded. "You go ahead. I'm going to grab my scissors and mirror."

Rissa hopped up and walked into the kitchen. She grabbed the bread and opened up the fridge. Barb showed her how to make simple things so she wouldn't starve. Her favorite, so far, was a turkey sandwich with hot cheese and mayo. Rissa threw it together and ate it standing up. She would need to make a list of her needs when she moved up to the cabin.

"You'll need to learn how to make hot food or use a microwave eventually." Barb smiled as she walked back into the room. She brought her supplies and a small trash can.

"If I live that long." Rissa took another bite of her sandwich.

Barb glared. "Listen, asshole."

Rissa nodded. "I find it interesting how I change from 'child' to 'asshole' depending on the subject matter." She took another bite and smiled around it.

"You know damn good and well I don't like you talking about dying, you little shit." Barb put her hands on her hips. "I like you for some unknown reason. Probably a defect in my wiring."

"Probably." Rissa put her empty plate down and grabbed an oatmeal cookie. She walked over to the couch and sat on the floor. "Chop away."

Barb sat down with a huff. "I'm going to cut off your cookie supply." She took the brush and a section of Rissa's hair.

"You may as well kill me."

The brush stopped.

Rissa held up her hands. "Small bad joke."

"I wasn't kidding about the cookies, smartass." Barb cut the section in her hand and took another. "I only have you for another couple days, and I'm worried. And you can tell me not to be, but I am." She paused. "Listen. I want you to meet Mandy. I've talked about you so much that she's being persistent about a visit."

Rissa turned her head.

"Damn it, Rissa." Barb dropped the section of hair she held.

"What in the fuck, Barb?" Rissa scowled. "Why don't you simply put a bomb in her bed? Come on! I shouldn't be anywhere near her. That's reckless."

"I can't explain it, but I think you need to meet her. She's hung up on meeting you. Every phone call and letter. She wants to meet my friend."

"Tell her no." Rissa's stomach turned at the thought of bringing Barb's child into her fucktastic life. "Absolutely not. No way."

"Think about it." Barb took another section of hair and pulled it toward her.

"I will not." Rissa crossed her arms and waited for Barb to finish. Helping her escape the facility and opening her home was one thing, but exposing a child to her? Rissa balked at the thought. She was death and destruction. A skull and crossbones. Barb should know better.

"There." Barb handed Rissa the mirror.

The red curtain of hair hung to her jawline, and Rissa approved. She could put a cap on and pass for a boy, if needed. "I like it." She passed the mirror back to Barb. "We're on for Thursday after work, right?"

CHAPTER 18

They planned on leaving as soon as Barb came home from work. Rissa now had toiletries and clothes to take with her. She would order more groceries when she arrived at the cabin. They would need to be careful, but Rissa kept her nose clean while she stayed at Barb's. No nocturnal visits, but she did find a few old friends.

Once she reached the cabin, Rissa needed to be extremely careful. She planned to stay for at least two months, if she lived that long. Rissa would tell the owner her parents died, and she needed a quiet place to sort herself out. There would be no visitors as she had no other family. Rissa simply required a place to be away from everyone. She hoped money silenced any other doubts he had.

They'd contacted him by phone and put a large down payment toward the rental. Rissa's cabin was the last on a dead-end road that pressed against the forest. She couldn't have asked for a better location.

There were so many variables to her possible suicide mission. Yes, there could be traps set up in the minds of her new targets. They could have expected something exactly like this to happen. On the other hand, maybe she was the first. Maybe they weren't prepared for a weapon to escape and then come back and fire at them. The last thought gave Rissa hope.

She told Barb the truth. There were tiers of vengeance. When Rissa reached the top and closest to the docs, she would have to be cautious. They would have protection, regardless of her living or dying. When former employees showed up dead and dismembered, it would raise all the red flags.

Then the hunt, the real hunt, would begin.

****

Barb came home after work Thursday and put her bags by the front door. She looked at Rissa, who sat on the couch with her bags packed. She dressed in jeans, hoodie, and white tennis shoes.

"I see you're eager to leave." Barb put her purse down and walked into the kitchen. "Don't even want a bite to eat?"

"Barb." Rissa looked up at the woman who gave her a second chance. Barb's back and shoulders stiff and unyielding. "It'll be easier if I go now. You bought enough groceries that I won't have to deal with that immediately."

Barb sighed, and her shoulders relaxed. She turned to look at Rissa. Her blue eyes filled with tears. "Why do you always have to make me cry?" She laughed a little and dabbed her eyes.

"I have no idea," Rissa answered truthfully.

The answer made Barb laugh harder. "I know you don't." She sighed. "Let me grab a drink, and we'll leave."

Rissa watched Barb make herself a soda and grabbed a water for Rissa. She took one of Rissa's bags and headed for the door. "Come on. Time's wasting."

Barb locked the door behind them, and they carried the bags to the dark blue compact she rented for this trip. She left her silver SUV at work and told her coworkers something was wrong with it. Rissa didn't want anything of Barb's connected with her, and that included a car with a traceable license plate.

They drove in silence, each in their own thoughts. Rissa wanted to wait a couple days before she made another visit. She wanted to settle into her own space and then work through her list. There were blanks, of course, but she hoped to fill them in as she went. Guards who knew other guards. Nurses who knew nurses and doc's names. It was a web of evil she planned to burn to the ground.

They reached the cabin's office in record time, and Rissa glanced at Barb before she climbed out of the car. "It'll only take a minute."

Barb nodded.

Rissa snagged her backpack and walked up the three steps to the front door. She pushed it open, and a small bell sounded.

There was a large desk in the one room filled with a laptop and two monitors. There were four baskets of various colors and assorted papers within. There was a large drink on an even larger coaster on the right side, and a middle-aged man who looked two decades younger smiled up at her.

"You Cary Allan?" He stood and offered his hand. "I'm Cain Hobbs. Pleased to meet you."

Rissa pushed down the alarm in her chest as the man offered his hand. She slowly took it. She needed to dial down the panic attack at the ready every time she became close to a new person. But Cain Hobbs incited more than a bit of fear. He stood well over six feet in jeans and a button-up shirt on a muscular frame. His dark eyes studied her, and she fought everything inside not to drop her eyes.

"Yes." She nodded. "I'm sorry. You're a bit intimidating."

Cain put his other hand on top of theirs and patted hers. "I'm sorry." He moved back. "I forget I'm built like a moose, and you're a petite package." Cain sat down. "You're here to pick up your key?"

"Yes." Rissa opened her backpack and removed her fake license. "Is it okay if I pay for another month right now? I need the time away. Everything is so loud, and I need the peace."

Cain's dark eyes softened as he took her license. "Yes, Ms. Allan. Perfectly fine. I'm sorry for your loss." He wrote down what he needed and handed the card back.

"I know it's not exactly safe, but I'm carrying some cash on me, is that okay?" Rissa counted out the bills and handed them to Mr. Hobbs.

He nodded. "I'm not picky about how I am paid, Ms. Allan." Cain took the bills, wrote her a receipt, and then handed her the key. "You let me know if you need anything." He handed her his card.

"Thank you so much." Rissa took the card and walked out of the office. She felt as though she were either going to pass out or throw up or both at the same time. Excitement battled nervousness. Rissa opened the car door, and slid back into her seat. She buckled up and blew out a breath.

Barb chuckled. "You look like a cat who swallowed a mouse."

"I don't know what I'm feeling." Rissa pressed her hand to her stomach. "I'm nervous, but I'm excited. I might throw up."

"Not in the rental car." Barb drove up the gravel road in the waning light. She passed three roads and finally turned left on the fourth. They wound through trees until they came upon the last cabin.

No one could call it friendly. It sat in the coming dark like a predator welcomed its prey. The shadowy forest clung to two sides of the structure with barely room to walk.

Barb drove up to it and kept her headlights on. "I'm glad you've never watched any scary movies."

"Barb." Rissa glanced at her. "I *am* the scary movie." She grabbed her backpack and walked to the front door of the cabin. Rissa slid the key in and turned the lock. She stepped inside and turned the alarm off. It was a perk she hadn't expected but one she appreciated.

Rissa walked back to the car and grabbed her other bags. She took them inside and came back out one more time. Rissa slid into the passenger seat and looked at Barb.

"You can't ever come back here."

Barb sniffed. "I know," she whispered.

Rissa looked at the woman who rescued her. The woman who fed, clothed, and took care of her. She felt a tightness in her chest she didn't understand. Fear? Regret? Rissa put her hand on Barb's right arm.

"Thank you, Barb."

Barb put her hand over Rissa's as tears streaked down her face. "If you can visit me, let me know. My door is always open."

Rissa took her hand back and nodded. She stepped out of the car and shut the door behind her. She walked inside and turned on the light. Rissa heard the car drive away and reset the alarm.

Alone.

The front door opened into a large living room with no break except a small island that separated the kitchen. There were two hallways, one on each side. There was a huge television across from the front door with two sitting areas. The kitchen shone silver in the overhead lights.

Rissa followed the closest hallway and found the bathroom on the right side. It was small but practical. She walked back out and farther down the hall was the bedroom. She followed the other hall and found the laundry room exactly opposite the bathroom. Rissa walked back into the living room and closed her eyes.

She felt better in the dark. Perhaps from years of having her eyes closed. Rissa cursed the facility but cut all lights except for a dim one over the sink. Much better. She unpacked and sorted everything into place. Barb went grocery shopping, and Rissa now had enough groceries for three or four days.

It would be time soon. Time to stretch her mind into the dark and tap on someone's door for a little visit. It was better than a cookie.

****

Rissa waited until nearly eleven before she closed her eyes on the big grey comfy couch and let her mind swim into the blankness. No one ever asked what it was like when she dream-walked. Too busy with instructions for murder. No one knew how beautiful or hideous it could be.

There were those with their minds wide open with brutal sights and sounds screaming and crying into the void. Minds with cracks in them where monsters begged to break free. Minds that made music when they moved and sounded like the wind with a song. Broken minds. Wistful minds. Malevolent minds. Quiet minds. Every mind with a different color and map.

Rissa slid through the darkness with a swiftness that left the usual cacophony behind as she focused on one thing: chocolate chip cookies.

Rissa concentrated on the taste and smell. The feel of the cookies in her mouth. Then she pressed into the dark and thought of the cook. The shadows shifted, and she stood in a massive kitchen with one facility foodie.

He wore an apron this time over sweatpants and a red t-shirt. He stirred something in a big pot on a stove and mumbled under his breath. Every once in a while, he would rub his bald head and throw something into the pot.

Rissa cleared her throat.

The cook turned, and his right hand trembled. "They said you would kill me." His brown eyes scared and searching. "I told them you wouldn't. They wanted me to have a guard, but I said no. Seems like the only one who could plant some shit in this old skull would be you. Are you going to kill me?" His voice shook.

"What the fuck? No!" Rissa touched his arm. "I wanted to thank you for all the meals you made. I doubt you knew for who you were cooking meals. Am I right?"

"Yes, girl." He turned off the stove and put the spoon down. "I'm Otis. You're Rissa. Let's have a seat." He led her into the living room. They sat on a large black sofa.

"You scared the hell right out of me the day your burst into my kitchen with that knife. I had no idea who you were or where you came from. What's this girl doing here, I wondered. No offense, but you looked like a druggie with the oversized clothes, pale skin, and desperate eyes."

"None taken."

"All hell done broke loose after that." Otis rubbed his head again. "The Boss mad as hell yelling about his weapon and incompetent staff and how he was going to kill you and how you were going to kill all of us." Otis shook his head. "Scared the shit right out of me. I had no idea what was going on there. I cooked. That was it." He blinked. "He gave us severance, asked if we needed guards, and burned that place to the ground."

"You didn't realize he meant a guard in your mind."

"Not at first." Otis made a face. "What kind of bullshit was this where I needed some trigger in my head because some girl was going to come and rearrange my brain? What shit had I gotten myself into?"

"They hurt me, Otis." Rissa looked into his eyes. "They hurt me in ways I'm not going to repeat to you. Do you believe me?"

"I do." Otis touched her hand. "I'm sorry, Rissa. My clueless old ass in the kitchen while they're sticking you full of needles."

"It's funny, Otis. The ones who didn't hurt me, apologize, while the ones who did, wouldn't think of it." She patted his hand. "Tell me about the guard Boss offered."

"Oh sure." Otis sighed. "Give me a second. It was stressful at the time. I don't want to miss anything." He closed his eyes.

"A day after you escaped, he met a handful of us at the coffee shop close by. He tried to tone down the whole 'keeping a young woman against her will' thing and stressed the fact you were dangerous and could hurt us. It sounded far-fetched. Boss said you could enter dreams and kill us. He offered for us to have a trigger implanted in our mind. When you appear, we activate the trigger, and you are closed in a room. It fills with poison, and you die."

"Wow." Rissa blinked. "FBI has nothing on this motherfucker." She looked at Otis. "Why didn't you take the trigger?"

"I'm not a killer." Otis sat up straight.

"I am." Rissa shook her head. "But thanks for not taking the plant. I'm not here to hurt you. I'm here to tell you that I'm not going to hurt you."

Otis smiled. "Thank you."

"Don't thank me." Rissa stood. "Now. Go back to stirring whatever the hell is in that pot."

Otis rose to his feet. "You're hard, child, but I suppose you've had to be. You be careful around the Boss and his boys. They're not playing, and they won't be happy until you're dead."

"Aware and noted." Rissa opened the door. "Same goes." She walked back into the black.

CHAPTER 19

Instinct.

Rissa could trust it a bit, after all. She had a list of her own to work through. Five more guards, three nurses, and three docs. She bared her teeth. No surprise the underhanded fucks ran scared. It pleased her they knew only enough to be terrified. Every night they went to bed, scared to dream. The simple fact fed Rissa's hunger. When she started her wave, they wouldn't know what hit them.

She eased out of sleep and padded into the kitchen for some ice water. Rissa used the fancy fridge and leaned against the kitchen sink. Buzzed from the visit, she made a sandwich and ate it standing up. The night, she thought. She claimed the night. They didn't stand a chance.

****

Sherri didn't frighten easily. She took a self-defense class. She carried pepper spray. Only mind invaders didn't give a ripe fuck about all that. They'd crawl into your brain like a fucking spider and lay eggs in your memories. She shuddered as she brushed her teeth. God, she hated that girl. Fucking mutant. They should have killed her when they had the chance. Shoot a little something extra in those veins. Shut her cold heart down to nothing. The thought brought a smile to her face.

Why are you smiling, Sherri? she asked herself. A big grin still plastered across her face.

Panic started somewhere in the pit of her stomach.

"Because it's funny, right? Dead mutant girl on the slab?" Sherri grinned wider in the mirror. She tried to stop but couldn't. Her hands gripped the sink as her toothbrush fell to the floor.

"Dead girls can't make spiders come out of your mouth, can they?" Sherri's mouth split wide open as a wolf spider walked out from her tongue and across her cheek. It scurried down her face and into the neck of her shirt. Two more followed and then a black widow.

Tears slid down Sherri's face as deadly spiders emerged from her mouth and slid down her body to bite and weave to their content. She lay on her bathroom floor. Sherri choked to death on her toothpaste. It was an odd way to go, but not odd if you knew a certain someone with a predilection for unusual murders.

Rissa woke in the dark with a wicked smile and the taste of toothpaste in her mouth. Funny what you sometimes brought back. Would the nurse's death sound the alarm? Yes, in a big way. More than Rajon's mishap ever would, if he shared with the class. Seemed to be each person on his/her own.

It also proved Rissa knew her way around the traps and triggers.

She stretched and blew out a breath. Middle of the night, and she needed something to soothe her. Rissa felt like she could light up the entire city. Maybe she *would* go to hell. Surely it wasn't a good thing she felt like this after a murder? Honestly, it didn't feel like a bad thing.

Rissa stood and grabbed an ice water. She drummed her fingers on the kitchen island and finally had enough. She threw on some jeans, tennis shoes, and a couple layers on top. Rissa grabbed her key, shoved it in her pocket, and stepped outside.

The porchlight shone only enough to illuminate the three steps leading up to the door. Three quarters of the cabin cloaked in darkness. Rissa stepped around to her left and walked into the woods. She brought the little pocket flashlight with her and turned it on.

Oh, it was gorgeous.

Rissa kept the light to the ground so she didn't fall and break something she would need later, but she had such a light step, she barely made an imprint. There were sounds in the night, and she wondered if she could dream of this forest and be part of it. It was the first fanciful thought she ever had, and it scared her. Rissa didn't play fanciful. She dealt in realism. There was nothing else.

She walked around for another half hour before she strolled back to the cabin. Rissa reveled in the fresh air and immediately made the decision to open the windows at the cabin. The cabin had the alarm system. It gave her a measure of security, and she hadn't seen another soul. That would change tomorrow with her grocery delivery, but she planned on being conveniently "absent" for that period of time. Rissa left instructions to leave the groceries on the porch.

Barb helped her set up a bank account and receive a debit card she could use to buy things. She showed Rissa how to use the disposable phone to find the grocery store and place her order. It was a lot of buttons. Rissa made sure to put Barb as the beneficiary on her bank account, if she wound up in a ditch somewhere. She didn't mention it to Barb.

Rissa unlocked the cabin and stepped inside. She reset the alarm and settled in. Rissa kept the cabin tight as a drum with the air on, but she wanted the windows open. Security warred with freedom, but security won. The thought of the windows open while she slept made her ill. Guess she would enjoy her fresh air in the middle of the night. Somehow appropriate.

Rissa would wait two days and then visit a guard. One right after the other was not only stupid, it was short-sighted. Staggering the deaths kept them off-kilter, and that's exactly what Rissa wanted. She wanted them to catch their breath right before she took it from them. Again. And again. And again.

****

The grocery guy dropped the bags off without hesitation and bumped his little car back down the gravel road with something close to music blaring.

Rissa waited until he was out of sight before she opened the door and brought them in. Did one usually become excited over groceries? She basically danced as she put them up. Her groceries. Her cabin. Her life.

The thought gave her pause.

Life.

That's what this was. Rissa glanced around. The thing she imagined if she weren't strapped down to a hospital bed. But... she couldn't simply forgive and forget, and she could thank them for that. Rissa knew she was a monster, but most children didn't start out that way. They took her. They trained her. They changed her.

What were they doing to the others? *The same? Worse?*

Rissa made herself a ham sandwich and examined the needle marks on her arm. Most so deep they would never heal. A permanent reminder of a temporary situation. She touched her wrists where red scars circled both. She had a matching pair on her ankles. There was a scar on her chin from the leather strap they used.

Cookies disappeared as she examined her legs. Her slight build worried her, and for the first time she noticed a couple of deep lines on each thigh. Odd. Razor, maybe? Rissa couldn't remember receiving the scars. She pulled up her shirt and looked at her hips and stomach. There was a scar far down on her left side she couldn't remember, either. Her chest and shoulders only held remnants of her trek to Barb's house.

Rissa sat on the couch and closed her eyes. Wonder if any of her targets took naps? What a fascinating thought. She let herself ride the waves into the darkness.

****

Mark Travers hated traveling with a passion he usually reserved for his favorite beer. But when all hell exploded at the facility, and the little bitch that could...did, it was time to change things up. He took Boss up on the offer of the trigger implant in his mind, but he also felt safer with a change of scenery.

Fuck Oklahoma. He took some of that severance money and hightailed it to Las Vegas. Anybody could get lost in that lousy-ass loud city. He landed and went directly to his hotel. Christ Almighty, he already had a headache.

Mark opened his room and let the bellboy stack his suitcases inside. He tipped him and locked the door. Beeline to the liquor cabinet, and he may live to see another day. Poured himself two fingers of bourbon and swallowed it down. God, that shit was smooth. He poured himself another and looked around.

The room was gaudy as fuck with mirrors and fake gold shit shining everywhere, but Mark finagled a deal for a two-week stay. They halved the cost of the room and threw in some free chips to throw around downstairs. He wasn't much of a gambler, but maybe if he got bored.

What Mark planned on doing was renting high-class company and having his dick sucked several times a day. He couldn't believe how much Boss gave them for severance. Sure, the little bitch was spooky as fuck-all, but she never saw any of them. And if she did come after him, she was in for a surprise. He'd enjoy this much-deserved vacation and go back when shit cooled off.

Rissa watched Mark from the largest shadow in the front room of his suite. She sat on a large end table and swung her legs back and forth. He was actually on the plane right now, snoozing off the four tequila shots he took at the airport before he boarded. He was a thin man with a gut that proved he loved beer and rich food. Small moustache. Balding brown hair. Beady green eyes.

She picked up the top of the bourbon decanter and hefted it in her hand. Solid weight, Rissa thought.

Mark collapsed on top of the bed and kicked his shoes off. *This was the life.* It was his last thought before Rissa shoved the glass lid down Mr. Travers throat.

****

Rissa opened her eyes slowly and allowed herself a smile. Rajon and Chet guarded together, but she wanted to save Chet for a rainy day. However, Mark? He liked to socialize. Rissa now had the name of the three other guards because the big boys liked to play poker on the weekends they weren't on shift. And surprise, surprise! No girlfriends or wives to say no.

Idiots. She snorted. They were stupid, but she couldn't be.

She opened a notebook she bought and made notes. Little black book of murders. Rissa jotted down the names of the guards with blank pages in-between each. She briefly wondered if Doc Brown Eyes still searched for her and what he used to do it. Did he think she died or killed herself? Or would he know she would come for him like she promised?

He would know.

Could he have someone similar to her at another facility? Rissa doubted it. If he did, she would already be dead. But there were many gifts out in the world, and he would twist any child with one to suit his purposes.

Nurses. Docs. Doc Bennett.

Rissa chewed on the end of her pen. Doc Bennett knew she would come. He would have every bit of his brain filled with landmines. Because she scared the shit out of him. The waiting. She smiled. The longer she waited, the more paranoid he would become. Let the motherfucker stew.

Safe Space Doc. Still didn't know his name, but she had the nurses, and they worked with him. Rissa wanted a little dialogue with the doctor who filed her reports. Would he be missing pieces or parts afterwards? Possibly.

Such a fine line between handling business but not rushing. Rissa needed to be methodical because when she confronted Doc Brown Eyes, she intended to hurt him in ways he never knew existed.

CHAPTER 20

Rissa fell into a routine. She woke around seven and made breakfast. Then she would nap, only sleep, until noon. Rissa ate lunch and then read for a couple of hours on her phone. She showered at two. Napped until six. Waited for dusk. Then she took her first journey into the woods. Rissa walked as far as she could in half an hour and marked trails and landmarks. She returned home and ate dinner. Next, she dream-walked. Sometimes she touched an employee and others she simply watched.

They fell into three groups.

She felt no need to harm any of the medics. Not only would that keep Barb safe from any suspicion, but none of the medics ever hurt her. They were only there, literally, to help. Did she appreciate they knew she was a prisoner and tortured daily? Not so much. Did they need the job financially? Yes. All of them. It wasn't her finest hour, but Rissa poked around in Barb's head one evening and took their names. There were four, including Barb. None knew what they signed up for, and none of them liked it.

That left guards, nurses, and docs.

Five of the six guards were sadists. Chet, being a stellar example. Two were racist brothers who worked together, and the other two were violent men who enjoyed being dressed out while they bullied others. Each had assault charges against them. Two had protective orders from girlfriends. It was a charming group. Rissa knew they would have a hair-trigger reaction to her presence.

Two nurses left. Rissa checked on both after Sherri's death.

A couple of quick peeks. Margot was in her fifties with an expensive red dye job and a lifelong nicotine habit. Tall and lean, she chain-smoked even in her dreams. Heavy makeup with a smoker's rasp, she sat in her brown leather recliner in her living room with a .45 in her lap. Rissa found it highly entertaining.

Margot died eating the .45 she kept so diligently at hand. The bullet took the top of her head and splattered it on the countertop behind her. Riss noted the grey hair underneath the dye job. She hoped the woman had a moment of recognition before all her memories were blown away. No pun intended.

Lauren, in her thirties, curvy and quiet. Long brown hair and light brown eyes. One would think butter wouldn't melt in her mouth, but wrong. Sweet Lauren enjoyed a level of violence that astounded Rissa. She dressed up and beat the every-loving shit out of people. Whips with spikes. Razors. Fists. Any way Lauren could leave a mark, she did. Woman missed her calling as a guard.

Rissa waited until Lauren called it a night, and then she treated Lauren to exactly what she loved. Took approximately six hours for the nurse to give up the ghost. No one would ever recognize her face again.

Ah, yes. The doctors. The ringmasters. Doc Bennett. Doc Brown Eyes. And Safe Space Doc now known as Dr. Chad Waters. Margot gave that up along with the fact she had a slight crush on the attractive younger doctor. Wonder how many crushes there would be when Rissa took his eyes or rearranged his face?

****

Rissa gave herself a break between visits. Sometimes five days. Sometimes a week. She only knew she could feel the time to strike and planned accordingly. Extra meals. Plenty of sleep during the day and walks in the woods at night.

While her body never seemed to grow stronger, both her mind and her talent did. Rissa honed what she had to an even deadlier tip. The smaller players fell away as the bigger players waited for their turn.

She hoped them smug. Rissa ate her turkey sandwich standing up. She hoped they thought they were better than her.

Oh, she hoped.

Barb messaged her on her last dummy phone and wanted to meet at the house. Rissa sighed. She had no doubt Barb would start the discussion about a visit with Mandy again.

It seemed senseless at best and a blood bath at worst.

Rissa didn't respond immediately and hoped Barb would catch the hint. Safe Space Doc's clock ticked closer and closer to a visit from one previous special patient.

****

Chadrick "Chad" Waters lived in a boring three-bedroom townhouse nestled up to the same. The grey roof did nothing for the red brick. There were no flowers planted or chimes hung. It looked drab and unremarkable.

Dr. Waters bought the house when he was young and simply didn't give a shit to worry about the aesthetic. Good price. Good neighborhood. What else did he need?

Chad didn't have any special interests besides data. Numbers in sequences. Numbers in charts. Numbers. Numbers. Numbers. People ranked low on Chad's interest. But specimens?

Come into my parlor...

The first time Rissa entered Chad's grey matter, she flinched. It wasn't the cold feel of apathy that touched her first, but the nearly inhumane way he treated everything.

She'd been first and foremost on the good doc's mind, and Rissa couldn't take back the image of herself, grey and gaunt, on the hospital bed in Hell Hall.

Safe Space Doc examined her as a bug through a microscope. He didn't particularly care if she had the proper nutrition or no. But the variables must remain the same. He didn't want his precious results skewed.

Doc Chad liked to push the patients to their limit. Harder push. Better numbers. More data. Push even more. Either the computer would spit out more figures, or the patient would expire.

So sorry. Moving on. Hook up the next.

Rissa read through doc's computer and his latest notebook. Sadistic nurse Lauren inflicted pain to those who wanted it. Sadistic Safe Space Doc inflicted pain to gain more knowledge.

Chad's findings soured Rissa's stomach. The sick motherfucker experimented on the housing insecure and desperate souls who needed quick cash.

He would stick a needle in anything for a number.

Rissa came to him as he stepped out of the shower. Shorter than Doc Brown Eyes but more muscular. Dark blue eyes and even darker brown hair cropped close to his skull. He didn't look like a doctor, at least not to Rissa. Or, she thought, the hundreds of people he duped.

Dark blue eyes flickered up as Chad grabbed a dark green towel to tie at his waist.

"Rissa." The word not a surprise nor a sigh but rather a declaration.

"Hey Chad." Rissa nodded her head. She studied him as he once studied her. Light green eyes scanned him in an instant, and she allowed herself a small smile.

"Really fucked up your data, didn't I?"

Chad's mouth tightened at her words. "My findings are incomplete."

Rissa clicked her tongue against her teeth. "Unfortunate."

Chad glanced through the bathroom door. "Can I at least dress?"

"No, Chad. You cannot." Rissa hissed out a breath. "This reunion train stops for no one."

"They're going to kill you." Chad tilted his head to the side. "And it's not going to be pleasant. Should have heard Boss man lose his shit when you left."

"How many triggers do you have, Chad?" Rissa pushed away from the doorframe and walked toward him. "One? Three? Six?" She paused and tapped her finger on her chin. "You would play the odds. Gather the statistics. Run a few 'what if' scenarios." Rissa motioned with her right hand.

Chad's eyes followed the movement.

Rissa plunged the serrated hunting knife so far into Chad, the blade broke on his spine. She leaned forward to his ear and twisted the knife to the right.

Pained moans escaped the good doc as his insides bled to the outside. Blood flowed freely from the stomach wound, and Rissa had to leverage herself to keep him propped up. "Bet those statistics never counted on a crazy bitch, did they?"

Rissa stood and kicked the knife farther in, but Doctor Chad never felt a thing. He'd left the world with five triggers untouched. He wanted answers. He wanted to know why. He wanted to finish his study.

But no. He never counted on a crazy bitch.

****

Rissa appeared back on her couch in the dim cabin and grabbed a plate from the fridge. She wolfed the ham sandwich down and opened a bag of chips. Those didn't last long, either.

When she finally felt balance again, Rissa marked Chad's name off her visitor list and studied the names left. She pulled Doc

Brown Eyes name from Chad's dying thoughts. Donovan Chase Fullbright III. Sounded like a right fucker, didn't he?

Rissa searched for Bennett for days with no luck. Maybe he had better fortune than most. Found a shield she couldn't penetrate.

She saved Chet for after Doctor Chad. Rissa wanted him to be scared of every shadow. She wanted that piece of shit to be as paranoid as possible. And triggers? Oh. She would bet that fucker was loaded with them.

And, finally, the one pulling the strings. All the strings. Finding these kids. Setting up labs. Rissa wanted only scorched earth left where these fuckers previously existed.

Her phone lit up with Barb's name and another message about meeting. Rissa sighed. She should go and meet Barb one more time. There were too many variables to guarantee another meet after she tied up the loose ends, if she made it that far.

CHAPTER 21

Barb and Rissa sat in the living room with pizza on their laps and soda nearby on the coffee table. Lights dimmed. Electronics off or silenced.

"I still don't understand why you wanted a kid." Rissa bit into the thick slice of pepperoni pizza and exhaled. Pizza. For life.

"You have a, rightfully, skewed perception of parents and children." Barb took a drink and looked at Rissa.

"I started the adoption process in my mid-twenties, but no one wanted to give a child to a single woman. It's ridiculous how many children need homes and reasons for not placing them. I passed the background check and filled out all the paperwork. I had testimonials from coworkers and friends. Didn't matter." Barb wiped away a tear. "I'd put in a new application every year. It broke my heart to be turned away."

"Why did you keep applying?" Rissa frowned.

"I wanted a child." Barb laughed at the look on Rissa's face. "I know you may not understand, but I felt as though I was missing something. I was missing a child."

Rissa simply stared.

"When I turned thirty-seven, I applied again. The woman at the adoption agency didn't even let me leave. It seems a girl was born prematurely with mental and physical issues. They didn't think she would make it, but would I take her?"

"That's fucking horrible." Rissa made a face. "Here. You want the dying child? Shit."

Barb sighed. "I agreed, of course. I went the next day and saw her in the NICU, where the babies go when they're not quite ready to leave." She smiled through the tears. "She was beautiful. Not quite four pounds. Peach fuzz on her head. They swaddled her tightly but told me her arms were not the same length and one foot looked like it turned in."

"You took the deformed and dying child."

Barb looked at Rissa sharply. Her blue eyes darkened. "I took the baby, Rissa. I loved her from the minute I saw her." She took a breath. "I know you don't understand. And I know why." Barb met her eyes. "But believe me when I say I wouldn't do anything different."

"Okay." Rissa took another bite of pizza.

"Mandy had to stay another two months in NICU for her lungs. I picked her up and brought her home at two months old, and I changed my life to fit hers." Barb motioned around. "It was easier when she was a baby. I would put her down and know where she was, but when she learned to walk, I thought I would lose my mind."

"Escape artist?"

"Basically." Barb blinked. "She walked with a bit of a limp and held her shorter arm closer to her body, and I swear to God, it gave her greater propulsion. I'd clean her up after breakfast, put her down, and I wouldn't even see the back of her when I turned around. Scared the shit out of me. I literally pinned a bell on her to keep track of where she went."

"Is that when you got rid of her?"

Barb glared at Rissa. "I'm going to give you a small break because you were literally raised in a fucking lab, but don't you ever say that to me again. Ever."

Rissa studied Barb's face and nodded.

"Mandy started school with the other kids with extra time

for speech. When the other kids had gym, she would have specialized therapy. I thought she enjoyed it, and maybe she did for a little while. But first grade made her miserable. It only highlighted the differences between her and the rest of the class. Mandy hated it. She wanted to climb a rope and read with her class. But her body didn't allow for that, and her speech still needed a lot of help."

"And the other kids?"

"They loved her." Barb smiled in remembrance. "Mandy is like a ray of sunshine. Everyone wants to be close to her. It's the funniest thing. Even the boys and girls the school usually had problems with? The ones I knew and were worried about? They friended her."

"Don't buy it." Rissa's lips tightened.

"No need." Barb smiled. "I want you to meet her. I think it's important you see my little girl."

"Gee, Barb. Think she'll cure all my ills? Wipe away all my troubles? Clear hundreds of those killings off my card?" Rissa faked a smile.

"I think Mandy is the complete opposite to everyone you've ever been exposed. I believe meeting her will give you a bit of a different perspective. It's not like I think she's going to change your whole life, Rissa. But how much damage could exposure to someone so sweet bring?"

"I could clutch my black heart and fall over from a heart attack."

"You really do need to shut up." Barb rolled her eyes.

****

Rissa still hated being out in the open. She lay in the back seat of Barb's silver CR-V and watched the lights and trees fly past. This world as strange to her as another planet. Rissa knew the basics but little else. Part of her wanted to sit up and scream at Barb to take her back. The thought of entering another facility tightened her body and made her stomach knot. Barb assured her none of the doors locked. Each of the residents wore a name tag with a built-in chip. Everyone except Mandy. Hers always died. She wore a bracelet like Barb's with her name on it and one bead that kept track of her whereabouts.

As much as she hated to admit it and never would, Rissa wanted to meet Barb's girl. Something inexplicable tugged at her.

The Live & Learn facility sat on fifty acres outside Oklahoma City. Doctors Shaw and Zimmerman started the facility ten years ago with a healthy grant and loads of research. Doctor Shaw's sister, Brandy, was developmentally disabled and grew up without the individualized help she needed. Dr. Ronald Shaw, and his good friend, Dr. Pryce Zimmerman, worked to create a place for those who would benefit from their research and time.

Dr. Shaw finally found his sister a healthy home for adults who needed a little help, and she thrived. He never wanted another child to wait as long as she did. They opened the first Live & Learn as a model and hoped to open two more in other states in the next five years. It was a dream come true.

"We're here."

Rissa could hear the smile in Barb's voice. She shoved her anxiety as far down as she could and sat up. "Why are all these places in the middle of fucking nowhere?" Rissa stared at the gigantic building that appeared more like a house than a hospital. The red brick and light blue-tiled roof spread out from left to right with windows and doors sporadically placed. Flowers bloomed at entrances, and trees provided shade for visitors.

"They let the residents run around outside and experience nature when the temperatures agree. Isn't it great?" Barb turned to grin at Rissa.

The words echoed in Rissa's mind as she recalled the first time her parents took her to Doc Hamilton's "school."

Barb's grin faded. "What's wrong? What did I say?"

"That's what the first doctor told my parents when they took me." Rissa stared at the foliage. "All the residents could go outside and play." She looked back at Barb. "I never stepped one foot on that fucking grass."

"I'm so sorry, Rissa." Barb blew out a breath. "I wish I could take back all the awful things in your life. All the shitty people and their bullshit promises."

"Are you sure you want a killer around your child?"

"I want *you* around my child, Rissa. You." Barb patted Rissa's hand. "I didn't drive two and a half hours to leave your ass in the car. Now hop out and meet my daughter."

Rissa allowed herself a small smile. "Yes, Barb."

They shut their car doors and walked to the front of the facility together. Barb opened the door and immediately took a small blonde jet to the stomach.

"Mandy!" Barb squeezed the girl tight and rained kisses down on her blonde head. "I missed you so much, lovebug."

A nurse walked up to them and laughed. "Hi, Barb! Your girl always knows. She's been watching the windows for the past half hour."

Mandy finally pushed away from her Mama and looked at Rissa.

They studied each other. Rissa noted the smaller arm, slightly bent leg, and large dark green eyes. Mandy wore a dress with cats playing with yarn. Socks with cats and yellow tennis shoes. Her long blonde hair free. It danced along her shoulders. Rissa wondered what Mandy saw.

"Wissa." Mandy held out her hand and looked up at Rissa.

Rissa blinked. She looked at Barb. "Huh?"

"Wissa." Mandy said it louder and hit Rissa's leg with her hand.

"I didn't say anything." Barb shook her head.

Rissa slowly slid her hand into Mandy's and let her lead them down the hall.

****

Mandy walked them to her room and made them sit down at the table in the middle. She brought out white paper and crayons and sat down between them.

"Mama." Mandy smiled at Barb.

"Yes, lovebug." Barb leaned over and kissed Mandy's forehead.

"Wissa." Mandy slid paper and crayons over to Rissa. She watched her expectantly.

Rissa took the supplies, and Mandy tapped the paper. Then she took her crayons and drew on her own page.

"Is this normal?" Rissa asked. She watched Mandy draw the sun slowly and carefully.

"We draw first. She insists. Mandy keeps all the drawings in her notebook." Barb drew a blue square.

"Did you tell her my name?"

Barb glanced up. "No."

Rissa's stomach sank as she glanced around the room. Nothing seemed strange or out of place. Mandy favored cats, and they decorated the walls and her bed. She had her own bathroom with a door, now open.

There was a large closed window by her bed with, you guessed it, cat curtains. Mandy had a dresser and shelf on the opposite wall. But something pricked at Rissa. She strained to hear, and that's when she realized she couldn't hear anything but waxy crayons on paper.

Rissa stood up from her chair and pushed it back with her legs. Panic swept through her. This was a trap. She should never have trusted anyone. Her eyes darted around the room, and she settled on breaking through the window by the bed when she felt a little hand slide into hers.

"Is okay." Mandy patted her hand softly. "I make quiet." She smiled crookedly.

Rissa stared at Barb. "Tell me what the fuck is going on. You have five seconds."

"Electronics die around Mandy. What you don't hear is any electric hum." Barb smiled at her daughter. "They keep her away from some parts of the facility on purpose, or their equipment may malfunction. It's the oddest thing."

Rissa's heart still raced. "No one is going to come and take me away?" She kept her eye on the window and braced herself.

"On my life." Barb sniffed. "I don't know how Mandy knows your name, but she seems to like you."

"If you lie to me…" Rissa began.

"I've let you meet my daughter, Rissa. Think about it. Why would I do that knowing you could kill us both?" She stared into Rissa's eyes. "This is my daughter."

Rissa blew out a breath and looked down at their joined hands. She squatted down to meet Mandy's eyes. "How did you know my name, Mandy?"

The little girl shrugged.

"Did someone tell you my name?"

Mandy nodded. "You."

Rissa led Mandy back to the table by her mother and sat down. "Do you know what I'm thinking right now, Mandy?" She stared into the little girl's eyes.

"No, but you look mad."

"I'm not. I promise." Rissa smiled at Mandy. "I don't understand.

That's it. But maybe I'll understand later." She looked at Barb. "Has she ever read your mind?"

"What?" Barb shook her head. "Never." She glanced at Mandy. "She's rough on electronics. That's her superpower." She chuckled.

Her superpower.

"We need a digital alarm clock." Rissa's mind raced. "Now. Please." She looked at Barb. "Small experiment. No one will be harmed. I only want to see what Mandy does to these electronics. Okay?"

Barb shrugged and stood. "Be right back."

Mandy smiled at Rissa. Rissa smiled back.

Barb returned with an old digital clock that looked like Herbert Hoover could have used it during his presidency. She shook it in her hand. "Best I got. A nurse on staff gave it up knowing they weren't getting it back. Mandy's reputation precedes her."

Rissa moved the table over to the wall and plugged in the ancient clock. It showed the correct date and time. She looked at Mandy. "What do you do to it?"

"It's loud." Mandy put her hands over her ears and blinked several times. "I make it quiet." She lifted her right hand and brought it straight down to her side. All the lights on the digital clock lit up at the same time, and then they all went out.

Dead as a doornail.

"The electricity is annoying. She said it sounds like a bug. When she's near a lot of it, she'll wear her headphones over her ears."

Rissa looked at Barb. "You realize that's not something every child can do, right?"

Barb walked over and hugged Mandy. "It's a small thing." She met Rissa's eyes. "It's not even in her chart. Her doctors feel it as nothing to do with her therapy here."

Rissa barely remembered her mother. But it's too bad she let her daughter fend for herself at the grand age of six and become the absolute paranoid mentally-ill shitshow she was today. Rissa glanced away. She still didn't understand how Mandy knew her name.

Mandy wriggled out of her mother's hug and walked over to Rissa. She patted her hand.

"You are soft hum." The girl closed her eyes and hummed softly. "Wissa is soft light and small hum. I hear your name in the sound." Mandy opened her eyes to stare up at Rissa.

Rissa pointed. "Does your mama hum?"

Mandy shook her head. "No." She brought Rissa's hand down. "You." Mandy patted it softly. Her bottle-green eyes looked into Rissa's. "You'll come see me again. Soon." She smiled.

"You heard the girl." Barb sat at the drawing table and looked at the offerings.

CHAPTER 22

Chet Green, piece of shit extraordinaire, prepared himself for a fight. Rissa entered his dream as a shadow and watched the sadistic guard ready himself for a war.

They never failed to amuse her. Guns? Knives? Rocket launchers? None of these mattered. The weapon, the best weapon, cocked in her head.

Would this asshole be loaded for bear in his grey matter? Of course he would. Chet wanted to be the hero in his own little play. Dressed like Rambo to annihilate everything in his path.

Said asshole sat on his bed with his back against the headboard. He dressed casually in a black t-shirt and dark blue jeans. Feet bare. Thousand-yard stare. Quite the tough guy. Rissa fought hard not to roll her eyes.

There were weapons placed all over the room. And that didn't count the booby-traps in the idiot's head. Chet currently had five knives strapped to various parts of his body. Guns and more knives placed strategically behind items or hidden in drawers.

Loaded for bear? Maybe. Prepared for Rissa? Not so much.

Rissa yawned, and Chet's head snapped toward the darkness.

He grinned. "I know you're there, you little bitch. Come out and play." Chet stood up from the bed and waited.

Rissa stepped from the shadow and crossed her arms. She examined Chet as he did the same.

"Bet you couldn't wait for me to arrive." Rissa glanced around the room but kept Chet in her peripheral. "Probably had a hard-on for days thinking about it." She met his gaze again.

"You should have died on that table." Chet sneered. "Look at you. Nothing but a pile of bones stitched together with hate and hubris."

Rissa smiled. "Come have a taste, you motherfucker." She waited. Knew the asshole would make the first move. He didn't disappoint.

Chet didn't say a word. He palmed a 9mm Glock and fired into her. The seventeen-round MAG bounced off her and into the surrounding walls. Chunks of plaster and wood exploded around her.

He lowered the gun, threw it to the side, and laughed. "I knew you wouldn't be that easy. Not the little girl who can pick a person's mind apart like peeling an orange."

Rissa simply studied him. She waited. And wasn't disappointed.

Chet pulled a silent trigger.

Rissa fell into darkness and landed on an enormous hospital bed with metal straps that immediately landed and latched her to the frame. A massive white light shone down on her while the rest of the room waited in shadows. Rissa centered herself and focused on ignoring the panic in her chest. The scenario expected but still triggered.

Chet appeared beside her with a shit-eating grin. "Back in the bed, little bitch. Told you it's where you belong." He reached down and lifted her chin up to meet his eyes. "You shouldn't mess with affairs you don't understand." He trailed his eyes down her body and snickered.

"Wasn't wrong about that 'pile of bones' remark. Have you actually lost weight being out in the big, bad world?" Chet's blue eyes lit up. "How about we have some fun before I turn you over to the boss?" He ran his hand down her bare leg. "I seem to remember promising you we'd play."

Rissa held in her revulsion and knew she would have to be quick. If Chet could trigger his mental bombs without a word, she needed to strike immediately.

"Do you want me to beg? Plead?" Rissa sneered. "You won't have the satisfaction." She spit in his direction.

"I'm going to break you, little bitch." Chet removed his shirt in one swift motion with a cruel smile. "I'm going to splinter you into little pieces and sweep them away without a second thought."

"Chet." Rissa's voice soft in the dark room.

"Hmm?" Chet worked on the button of his jeans and didn't bother to look up. If he did, his priorities may have shifted a bit.

Chet Green, ironically, didn't like being held down or constrained. A sixth-grade bully blocked him into a corner when he was in third-grade and stuck his hand down Chet's pants. The abuse seemed to last forever as the older kid pinned him and blocked his air. All Chet would forever feel is the boy's hot breath and wandering hand.

Rissa now sat up and watched her abuser unzip dark jeans. She cleared her throat.

Chet's head snapped, but it was too late to realize the consequences. Rissa swung a two-pound kettlebell neatly into Chet's jaw, and he crumpled without a sound.

Rissa peered over the side of the bed at the unconscious man and helped herself to the twisted thing he called a brain.

****

Rissa watched Chet wake slowly with a groan. She pinned him against the wall in a nice X with arms and legs free to explore as she wanted.

His head lolled on his chest until he shook it with a bit more force and squinted his eyes open. Chet's face hardened.

"You *were* loaded, weren't you?" Rissa materialized a metal chair and sat on it. "Your little brain seethed with landmines. Eager to shut me down and prove you're the big boy, after all."

"Fuck you," Chet snarled.

"Fuck me?" Rissa snorted. "You have jokes." She studied him. "I thought about what I wanted to do to you." Rissa rested her chin on her hand. "Drop you off a cliff. Drown you in an ocean. Car accident." She sighed. "But you're special, Chet. You said so yourself. I had to think on it for days." Rissa stood up from her chair and walked toward the pinned man.

"How many years was I there? How many bones did you break? You left bruises on me that didn't fade because you always gave me more."

Rissa clucked her tongue. "Pure brutality." She stared into Chet's eyes. "That's what you respond to, isn't it? What you watch all alone in that shithole you call a house. What gets you off. What makes you feel invincible."

"They're going to find you, and it's going to be glorious. No more meal trays. They'll feed you through an IV. No more toilet. You'll have a bed pan." Chet smiled. "Kill me, then. I'll haunt your ass for an eternity."

Rissa bit her lip to stop it, but she couldn't. She threw back her head and laughed. Cackled until she nearly vomited. The tears and the spit mingled while Rissa tried to regain her composure.

"You." She raised her hand to point. "You idiot." Rissa snorted and wiped her face. "Thanks for that. Needed it." She walked over to Chet and waved her hand. A ball gag appeared in his mouth, and Rissa nodded in satisfaction. She examined him. "You've one more trigger. A sweet little bomb that detonates when you die. Couldn't defuse that one."

Chet's eyes widened.

"I *am* a pile of bones." Rissa held up her arms, scarred and small.

"I am a living memory of what that lab did to me." She paused. "But I'm not weak nor stupid." Rissa palmed a #10 scalpel blade with the smallest smile. "I am, however, one pissed-off woman."

The first cut sliced into the tender flesh on the top of Chet's right foot. He winced and tried to withdraw the innocent skin.

"We're going to play a game called 'Blades and Bruises', Chet." Rissa watched the blood slide down the instep of Chet's foot and drip slowly onto the floor. "One side for blades. One side for bruises."

Rissa's eyes met Chet's again. "Winner walks out." She paused. "Loser...doesn't."

Blue eyes widened in comprehension. Yes. The first cut stung. But there would be many, many more.

Rissa held out her hand, and a bright red kettlebell appeared. She swung down, onto the other foot, and heard what some would describe as the snapping of a dozen glow sticks.

Chet moaned as tears skimmed down his face, and he fought the restraints.

Rissa eyed the maimed foot and nodded. "Bruises might win. Wasn't really sure. Probably more of a game of where I decide to slice and dice next." She raised her head. "Anything you want to say, Chet?" Rissa moved the ball gag with a thought.

"YOU FUCKING CUNT!"

Rissa blinked. "Be that as it may..." she trailed off. The ball gag reappeared in Chet's mouth. She held up the scalpel and took another swipe.

****

The biggest and baddest guard on the block, Chet Green, now hung limply on the once-white wall. Skin sliced, on his right side, every inch or so while blood clotted or dripped down from his fingers to his toes. The scent of copper filled the air, and Rissa breathed through her mouth.

Chet's left side didn't fare well, either. Black eye. Broken nose. No usable appendages. Cracked ribs.

The writing, and Chet's broken body, on the wall. He wouldn't be walking anywhere, much less escaping this nightmare.

Rissa didn't find enjoyment in dishing out the punishment Chet richly deserved. To her, it was simple. You hurt them before they had a chance to hurt you. Again.

She stepped close for the last time and removed the ball gag.

Blood dripped from Chet's mouth as Rissa was sure he bit his tongue more than once. His eye rolled back in his head, and he mumbled against his chest.

"The finale is upon us, Chet." Rissa stared impassively at the lump of flesh in front of her. "You've been a sport, but I have other things to do."

"You're..." words mumbled to mush as Chet fought to say one last thing.

Rissa had no fear of moving closer as Chet's inability to travel anywhere ceased an hour ago. She ducked her head close to the bloody mouth.

"Ttttt...wins..." The word fell and shattered between them. Chet tried to smile but only winced.

Rissa drove her scalpel into his carotid artery, on the left side, of course, and watched Chet expire. The force of the blast threw Rissa against the far wall, and she blew out a breath as her shield disintegrated. Real games. Real consequences. Pieces of Chet scattered from floor to ceiling. She threw the weapons into the wind and woke up.

Twins.

The sisters.

What about them?

Rissa sat up on her couch and focused. They were the payback for not killing the young genius.

Payback.

The word rung in Rissa's head like an obnoxious church bell. Payback. Payback. Payback.

CHAPTER 23

"How did they teach a child to kill?"

The words both simple and horrifying.

Rissa exhaled and grabbed another chocolate chip cookie. "You sure you want to know this, Barb? You may have problems sleeping afterward."

"I think I do." Barb's blue eyes softened.

"Be sure," Rissa warned. She tucked her crossed legs close. "You can't unring a bell."

"Tell me."

"They triggered me with anger in the beginning." Rissa spoke with no inflection.

"Wow." Barb made a face. "That doesn't seem like the brightest move."

"I was a child. I didn't have a palate of emotions of them to play off. The best realization ever was finding out empathy is usually in a child's toolbox around ages six to seven. No exposure. That would have royally fucked up their shit. Can you imagine?" Rissa grabbed an imaginary microphone and lowered her voice. "Tear up that green monster with the blue eyes. Rip it to shreds." She rolled her eyes. "And then me, 'but what if it's sad?' Can you imagine?"

Barb sighed. "You've lost so much."

Rissa shrugged. "Serial killers can't have sleepovers." She tilted her head. "That's the new title of my biography. It's perfect."

"Rissa!"

"It shocks you when I say it even though we both know it's the truth." Rissa sat up straight and looked Barb in the eye. "I'm a serial killer. I was a child once, yes. But now I'm an adult. I've killed hundreds of people, Barb. Hundreds. They had families. I took that from them."

"I know." Barb lightly touched Rissa's knee. "But most serial killers aren't underweight teenagers with track marks and permanent scarring from being strapped down to a fucking hospital bed."

"I'm not arguing over semantics."

"Oh, shut up!" Barb stuck out her tongue. "You're impossible."

****

Rissa needed to try and contact one other person. They could be dead. Odds were good for it. But if they were still alive, Rissa required their assistance.

She closed her eyes and drifted. Back to that night. Back to someone she'd forgotten as quickly as possible. Rissa wondered if they remembered.

The room came into focus slowly. Not a room, exactly, but a long metal tunnel with electronics plastered together on the far wall. The near wall held hooks for clothes, two refrigerators, and miles of a maze where people milled.

He sat in the center of the computer melee while his fingers moved lovingly over the keyboard. The light above adequate, but the real light shone on the young man's face and illuminated the army of screens before him.

"You didn't die horribly on the streets?" Rissa looked around the massive area and bit back her smile.

He spun around then.

Rissa could still see the boy in him. The cocksure look. The lanky build. GENIUS still clearly stamped on his forehead. That forehead also held a nice three-inch scar from left temple to middle part. The price to pay for being young on the streets with no one but himself. At least, the price she could see.

The grin widened first. "Contrary to popular opinion, I did not." Kase spun around in his chair to look at Rissa. "You look like shit, though."

"That serial killer lifestyle." Rissa crossed her arms. "Hell on the body and mind."

Kase jumped up from his chair and pulled her into a hug. "You're a sight for sore eyes, white girl." He moved back a bit. "Didn't think we'd meet again."

Rissa looked up into his eyes. "You've done well for yourself, genius. You ever figure that light thing out?"

"Small potatoes." Kase put his arm around her shoulders. "Walk with me, ma petite."

"Oh, shit. Someone pull Kase back. He's on the brag block. Save the skinny white girl." A young girl walked by and rolled her eyes at Kase.

He swatted at her. "Show some respect, Penny. This is she." He emphasized the pronoun.

Everything stopped in the space.

Rissa glared up at Kase. "Seriously."

Kase winced.

Penny studied Rissa. "This is the urban legend." Her dark brown eyes never wavered. "This is the dream walker. The girl who saved your ass. The one who escaped from the unescapable." The smile spread across her face. "Well, shit, girl! Make this asshole properly introduce you next time. We've been dying to meet you!"

The voices started up again, and Kase waved his hands in the air. "Rissa, understandably, becomes overwhelmed easily. Do not mob her. Show respect."

"Do not tap on the glass cage," Rissa muttered.

"Hey." Kase looked down at her. "None of that. You broke out of that fucking place. You saved my life." He nodded with his head. "I saved theirs. Now," he continued, "let me brag."

"Are you all riding the same wavelength?" Rissa frowned. "I didn't expect a party when I arrived."

"Cool, huh?" Kase blew out a breath. "Took me fucking forever to onboard likeminded people. Then I worked for that trust in the only way I knew how."

"You showed them magic." Rissa looked at him in wonder. "You told them about me."

Kase nodded. "It was all I had, at the time. Not all at once, but I had to pull the rabbit out of the hat." He rubbed the scar on his forehead. "Rough start, but I eased myself into street life."

"You ran drugs."

He shrugged. "You go with what you've got. And there's a lot of money to be made in it." Kase frowned. "Hated it, though. I upped my game and began to let others know I could run numbers."

"Oh, shit." Rissa allowed herself a smile. "Now, that's more up your alley." She studied him. "How many managers approached you?"

"Four." Kase blew out a breath. "Thought I would throw up on the first one. Motherfucker big as hell with chains and shit. Fist bigger than my head. Didn't think I would make it out of the meeting." He smiled in remembrance. "Top Dog. That's what his boss called him. We still keep in touch."

"Of course, you do." Rissa rolled her eyes.

"That crew bankrolled this." Kase held out his right arm and swept it back toward himself. "I worked my ass off for two years. Kept my bankroll on the down low. Gave them a replacement to leave the life. That, and some of my hard-earned money." Kase blew out a breath. "Worth every fucking penny."

"What did you build, Kase?" Rissa looked around, absolutely clueless but hopeful.

"Ah, my dear one, what *didn't* I build?" Kase grinned. "Kept my 'light' idea but improved on it." He pointed above them. "Less electricity than refrigerators use. Always on."

Kase escorted Rissa to a chair at a separate table, away from the cacophony of computers. He watched her with sharp eyes. "You want something."

"I need something."

"Name it." No hesitation.

"I need you to help me destroy a man and his life's work."

"Give me the details, and I'll come up with something brilliant. I'll have a courier drop it off at whatever location you choose." Kase pulled out a tablet and tapped away on it. He nodded to himself and placed it between them. Rissa filled in the details.

"Maybe someday you and I can meet face-to-face instead of these nocturnal reunions." Kase held up a hand. "I know the risks, Rissa. I calculate them daily when I do business. I'm ass-deep in shit even *I* don't talk about aloud." Brown eyes studied her. "You literally saved my life."

"What kind of person would I be to put that life in jeopardy?" Rissa sat back and folded her arms across her chest. "I now know your home address." She glanced around. "We can talk like this."

Kase paused and his fingers danced over the table top while he struggled for words. "You ever need anything…" he trailed off,

"...I better be the first person you ask."

Rissa smiled and stood up. "You're in the top three."

She disappeared in an instant and woke up at the cabin. Rissa remembered the beating Doc Brown Eyes gave her when she "failed" Kase's mission. Now, that failed mission basically ran the world from an underground tunnel.

Kase, and others like him, threatened society when they didn't adhere to the rules and regulations of the privileged and influential. They thought, and fought, freely.

Certain circles wanted to own them. Control them. Silence them. Break them. If you could not make these free thinkers submit, then they were of no use.

Destroy them.

Rissa rose from the couch and made herself a lemonade. She sipped the tart liquid slowly and developed a plan to use Kase's offering to upset the status quo.

CHAPTER 24

Donovan Chase Fullbright III walked downstairs to his study. It was late, but he had an idea for the latest facility. Since they'd lost Rissa, he'd brainstormed better ways to build his mouse trap. She'd been wily, that one. Her petite frame fooled him into thinking she was frail. His mistake. One he wouldn't make again. There were already big plans in place for another facility in the sticks of Oklahoma. He sent feelers out for "special" children. Rissa may have been one of a kind, but he knew there were others to harvest.

The slight buzz of his alarm system soothed him as he reached the bottom of the stairs and glanced outside his floor-to-ceiling windows. Donovan enjoyed the night. The quiet reflection of the day. The silent reverie. He did miss the murdering, though. The power over someone's life was the reason he became a doctor. When the usual practices bored him, he found his home with Sunmos Lab.

They were visionaries. They saw the future outside the normal ways and means. Donovan didn't know there were people who could move objects with their mind or read someone's thoughts. He sure as hell didn't know about a little girl who could kill people in their dreams. Rissa fascinated him from the beginning. She killed Hamilton with no remorse, and he savored it. He could thank Hamilton for one thing, and it was taking her at the right age. Children learned empathy around seven or eight. Rissa bypassed that completely. It made her a fantastic weapon until she decided to rebel.

How could he know the little bitch plotted and planned?

Donovan purposely kept her nutrition at a level to keep her alive, little else. But her mind...her fucking mind...he should have known better. Enough of self-recrimination. Work continued on the next project. He walked into his study and turned on the light.

"Hello, Donnie. Cool pajamas."

Rissa enjoyed the way Doc stopped in his tracks like a deer in headlights. He attempted to walk, but she waved her hand, and he stilled.

She sat at his desk while her feet rested comfortably on top of it. Rissa admired the room full of steel and wood. Behind her rose a massive bookcase and a portrait of the Milky Way. To her right, steel shelving with framed documents, and to her left, an open door where one unsuspecting piece of shit entered in rather boring light blue and white striped pajamas.

Directly in front of her, windows showed the night. Rissa appeared more than a few minutes ago and made herself comfortable. This was Doc's domicile. His safe place. She wanted to leave her fingerprints all over it. And him.

"Have a seat, Donnie." Rissa pointed to a seat across from her. He shuffled over to it and sat. She winked. "You want so badly to reach that trigger, don't you?" Rissa sat up. "But you can't because I won't let you. You're stuck to that chair in body and mind as much as I was strapped down to that fucking hospital bed, you motherfucker."

Rissa stood, walked over to his side of the desk, and sat down on it. She studied the man in front of her. "What is it you told me, Doc? This would never happen?" Rissa slapped him. "Oh, it's happening."

She admired her handprint on his cheek. "You thought you were safe in this humming little house, didn't you?" Rissa shook her head. "You didn't share info with any of the others that it may help them survive." She tilted her head. "It wouldn't have, but that's not the point. You're a selfish fuck, and you're going to pay for what you've done."

"How did you bypass my alarm?"

"Oh. That cool humming, we both hear? The same shit you used at the facility to jam my dream walking?" Rissa shrugged. "You don't need to know. You only need to know it didn't and doesn't stop me. My small ass staring at you right now proves the point."

"You'll kill me."

"Am I that predictable?" Rissa sighed. She hopped off the desk and walked back around. She turned on the computer and typed in his password. "One good thing about thumbing through your mind is all this knowledge about a new facility." She glanced over at him. "I'll cut you to pieces while you're still alive before I let that happen." Rissa smiled and typed some more.

"I have the list of everyone you've ever killed."

"Awesome, you fucker. So do I." Rissa tapped her forehead. "You think you're smarter than everyone. You think the fact you've got traps in your brain for me will shut me down. You think the traps on this computer will stop me." She watched Doc's face change for the first time to the tiniest bit of fear. "Oh. You thought I came in blind? Guns blazing and mouth shooting off? Christ, you dumb fuck, I'm not you." Rissa typed in a few more things and looked up.

"What are you doing?"

"Who? Me?" Rissa pointed to herself. "I put a kill switch on your computer which will wipe the hard drive and everything on it. Bonus…it's sending an email to everyone in your contact list and doing the same to their computers. It's a nasty little bug a friend of mine came up with to help me out." Rissa walked back to the doc. "Now. You're thinking your friends at Sunmos probably have a building full of servers with backed up information they can simply grab again and implement their fucked-up schemes with children." She rolled her eyes. "Bad people are incredibly obvious."

"They're prepared for people like you."

"Like me? Probably. Like my uber brilliant techie friend? I doubt it." Rissa shrugged. "Now." She hopped back on the desk. "Let's chat."

Doc glared at her.

"People are not property, Donnie. You keep acting like it's your right to scoop them up and make them do your bidding." Rissa shook her finger back and forth. "That's why you're in trouble right now. You make bad choices. Were you not loved enough growing up?"

"What do you want, Red? You want to torture me? Do it. You want to rip me to shreds? Do it. But you can't stop my research. You can't stop what I've put in motion." He grinned up at her. "You were a fucking gold mine."

Rissa studied him. She felt the trap. Felt it as sure as if he were breathing down the back of her neck. The words "gold mine" echoed between them.

Doc waited a full minute before he spoke. "You're a natural born killer." A 9mm appeared in his right hand, and he raised the barrel to Rissa's face. She kicked it with her left foot, and it shot into the ceiling.

He sprang from his chair, and she swung her right leg into his jaw and knocked him to the floor. Doc fired up at her twice. Rissa jumped behind the desk and lowered herself to the floor to watch his feet. She palmed a .45 from nowhere and shot his left ankle.

The howl of pain brought a smile to her face, and Rissa scooted around to the side of the desk to see her prey.

Doc Donnie lay on his right side and clutched his left leg to his chest. Blood poured out of his shattered left ankle while bone fragments appeared as small, bloody-white spears.

Rissa stood up and shot a hole through the middle of Doc's right hand, and he jerked it toward his chest, also. The 9mm pinwheeled away from him. She looked down at the trembling man in the fetal position.

"You know. Not once did I ever cower in front of you. I would have pulled my heart out of my chest before giving you the satisfaction." Rissa kicked him in the groin.

Doc pulled his entire body back and tried to make himself smaller.

"Is this what you've always been? A small man behind a clipboard? A man who hurts children and murders for money?" Rissa's rage lit like gasoline-soaked kindling. She stretched out her right hand, and her fingers thinned into eighteen-gauge needles. "How many times did you take me under, Donnie? How many needles have you shoved into my veins?" Rissa stood over his left side and thrust the needles on her right hand deep into Doc's leg.

Doc screamed in pain and tried to move her with his left hand. Rissa pulled the needles out and watched in satisfaction as blood soaked through his pant leg. Rissa repeated the motion four more times before she pulled back and spit on him.

Donnie moaned and cried on the floor while blood pooled around his body. He pawed softly at the marble with his right hand, and tried to crawl away.

Rissa stepped away and leveled her back against the farthest bookcase. "Come on out, Donnie. I'm not going away. Your little puppet has been fun, I have to admit. But I'm not leaving until you bring your sorry ass down here. Or I can come up there." She looked around the room and cocked her head to listen.

"What are you scared of, Donnie? Other than me disemboweling you and making you watch?" Rissa's eyes changed color for a minute. "Oh." She blinked and then grinned with all her teeth. "Who's afraid of little ol' me, Donnie?" The grin slid from Rissa's face. "You should be."

"You hid behind a mask for a decade. You tortured and abused me to control me. I was never a person. I was a weapon. Something for you to point and shoot." Rissa took her first two fingers of her right hand, put them together, and pointed. Then she pulled her thumb up, to cock the gun.

"Come out now and face me, you lowlife motherfucker, or I will spray this entire room with bullets, and you can taste your own fucking teeth."

Doc appeared at the bottom of the stairs. The groaning pool of blood disappeared without a trace.

"You're a bit unsettling." He walked toward her but stopped in the open door.

"Are you unsettled?" Rissa kept her right hand formed into a gun.

"More than I care to be."

"Ah. There's the self-important piece of shit I recognize. Glad you could join me." Rissa lowered her hand. "Did you think you could fool me with that pathetic doppelgänger? He didn't even try to kick me or grab my leg." She rolled her eyes.

"Maybe I'll send you duplicates all night." Doc came in and sat down across from the desk.

"Maybe I'll rip your balls off and feed them to you." Rissa walked over and sat facing him. She smiled. "You said it, yourself. Awake? I'm simply an underweight mouthy teenager. Nothing special there." Rissa paused. "But dreamland? This is my domain. I have the power here. You're in my web, Donnie."

"Let's bargain."

"There is literally nothing for you to bargain. I'm here to destroy you and for everything you stand." Rissa made a face and shook her head. "Do you really buy into your own delusion? Do you honestly think that a woman you tortured to do your bidding would even *consider* bargaining with you?"

"Your mother's alive."

"And?" Rissa shrugged. "That bitch left me to the wolves. Don't give two fucks. She may as well be dead."

Doc paused.

"Oh." Rissa blinked. "That was your big one, wasn't it? Did you forget I'm trained to not care? That you and the other sick fucks made me into this?" She slammed her hands on the desk hard enough to make Donnie jump. "Fucked that one up, didn't you?"

"There's no point in killing me. You've already wiped my computer and set your virus free." He glared at her.

"No point?" Rissa stood up and leaned over the desk. She stared hard at the piece of shit who took her life away. "There's no point in letting you breathe one more second on this earth. No point in letting your fucked-up ass have one more chance at another child. No. Point."

"Then kill me," he hissed. "Do your fucking job, Red. Isn't this what you promised me years ago?"

Rissa walked around the side of the desk and sat on it while her legs dangled next to Doc Donnie.

"You do have a way with words, Donnie." Rissa nodded. "But I've decided not to go that route." She smiled wide. "There's another permanent solution right in front of me, you could say. Simply *beckoning* me."

"No." Doc shook his head. "No, no, no, no, no, no," he moaned.

Rissa held up her hand, and Doc's head stilled mid-motion. Those brown eyes terrified and glazed over.

"Going to tippy-tap into that little brain of yours and do some rearranging." Rissa right finger circled his temple. "Then you won't know what you don't know." She pressed harder, and her eyes changed to brown. "Look at this frontal lobe," she purred. "Let's make a few changes."

CHAPTER 25

Rissa woke up and felt refreshed. She threw her covers back and stretched. All her problems weren't solved, but her to-do list shrank. Doc Donnie killed Bennett because he wouldn't keep his scared mouth shut. Trash took out trash.

Rissa found an acquaintance of Doc Donnie and planted the suggestion to check on him. To everyone else, it looked like Donnie had a stroke. Rissa turned his frontal lobe into madness. All higher cognitive functions gone. A nurse would feed him with a baby spoon the rest of his life.

She thought about Kase's kill switch and the damage it did. Rissa trusted him implicitly. If he said it disabled the beast, then it did. She would check back with him later for all the details. They would need to sweep in and rescue the children.

Details.

Plans.

The children may be…difficult.

Rissa hated the thought she may have been the prototype for capturing and/or keeping children as weapons. She hadn't had a choice, but it still pissed her off.

She hopped out of bed and walked into the kitchen to make a sandwich. A celebratory turkey, hot cheese, and mayo on wheat. Rissa grabbed some plain chips and sat on the couch.

What would she do when she finished rescuing children and dealing with bad people? Rissa took a bite of her sandwich and chewed slowly. Freedom was no longer a wish but a reality.

Could she buy this cabin from Cain or maybe have one built farther back in the woods?

Rissa wanted nothing to do with the public at large. It was an overwhelming and generally terrifying thought. She wanted to live peacefully. Quietly. Read her books. Study the stars. Walk in the woods. Eat her sandwiches.

Forget.

Forget the needles. The blood. The faces of the souls she took. The pain. The constant fear.

She placed her sandwich back on the plate. Rissa couldn't control the memories. Couldn't scramble her own brains and hide the bad things. Maybe they would lessen over time.

Maybe.

****

Barb wanted Rissa to call her as soon as she had the chance. The older woman worried about her, which she didn't quite understand. They still took precautions with burner phones. Rissa trusted nothing.

Rissa called, and Barb offered to come get her so they could visit Mandy together. Rissa told her she'd walk down as she needed the exercise. Barb protested, but Rissa threatened not to come so she backed down. Rissa hung up the phone.

She liked Mandy. That girl was fire in a bottle. Lively. Funny. With her own superpower. Rissa pondered over it more than a few times. How many kids could do things others could not? And how vulnerable and dangerous did that make them?

Barb protected Mandy, and her caretakers didn't seem to care that Mandy could kill the power on damn near anything. They simply worked around her. Rissa hoped, that for everyone involved, it stayed that way.

Rissa threw on some jeans, an oversized dark grey shirt, and some grey tennis shoes. She grabbed a white ballcap and put it on. Warm outside so she didn't need a jacket, but she had a thin long-sleeved shirt under her oversized one. The scars on her arms would always need to be covered up. They invited looks and questions she didn't want.

She set the alarm on the cabin and walked out into the morning sun. Rissa spent years in a cold building that reeked of bleach. Every day she spent in fresh air felt amazing. She would never take for granted the sights or smells.

It took her a little over an hour to reach Barb's house, and Rissa still used every bit of precaution as if it were the first time. A wily rabbit was a safe rabbit. She skirted the woods and examined the house for several minutes before she took the back side again. A quick turn of the knob, and she was in.

"Good timing!" Barb yelled from the kitchen. "Cookies came out five minutes ago. First batch already cooled."

Rissa smiled and walked down the hall into the kitchen. She grabbed the largest peanut butter cookie she saw and stuffed it into her mouth.

Barb shook her finger. "You better not choke. I'm not giving you the Heimlich."

Rissa chewed happily and studied the older woman. Barb seemed to have aged a bit. More grey in the dirty blonde than before. More lines around the eyes. But the same smile that welcomed Rissa more than a month before.

"Glad to see you, child." Barb patted her on the head in lieu of a hug. "Toss about a dozen of those in a big baggie, please. I need to throw on some clothes, and we'll be ready."

Rissa looked at her billowy orange and yellow dress. "You're not wearing that?"

Barb laughed. "These clothes are not for public consumption." She shook her head and walked back to her bedroom.

Rissa grabbed another cookie and took a big bite. She eyed the rest of them and hoped to hell they were going home with her. Part of her wanted to shove them in a baggie and hide them for later. Barb told her it was only natural since she couldn't keep anything for herself at the facility. But Barb would make sure Rissa would have her own things, and she trusted Barb a bit.

That came in handy at her next words.

"Going to see Mandy's biological mother today."

Rissa paused mid-bite. "The hell did you say?" She glanced up toward the hall.

"You, me, and Mandy on a road trip." Barb came back from her bedroom with a bright pink flowery sundress and white sandals.

"Are you high?" Rissa stood up. "Sampling the goods at work?" Disbelief showed in her voice. "Why don't I simply hang my ass out the window of your car and let everyone know where I am?"

"Rissa." Barb sighed. "It's a small assisted-living center. No one cares about your ass."

"Everyone cares about my ass." Rissa shoved the rest of the cookie in her mouth and chewed quickly. "In fact, I would bet my ass is wanted all over the United States." She frowned. "Maybe even foreign countries."

"I've done everything you told me to do." Barb pulled her greying hair into a loose bun and patted it softly. "We disappeared for a bit. Came back. Watched for followers. The lab contacted me once to ask how I managed, and I told them I live in fear every day."

Barb glanced at Rissa. "True. But I don't live in fear of them. I worry for you."

"Ick." Rissa grabbed another cookie and shoved it in her mouth.

"And my grocery bill for all those ten pound sugar bags." Barb shot her a look and smile.

"I can pay you back." Rissa already had her hand in her pocket.

"The hell you will." Barb frowned. "If anybody in this world needs cookies, it's you."

"Will not dispute." Rissa removed her hand. She studied Barb. "Why do I need to go?"

"Honestly?" Barb looked around for her purse. "Mandy was adamant about it."

Rissa picked up the partly-obscured straw purse behind the pillow and dangled it in the air. "Looking for this?"

Barb grabbed it with a laugh. "Yes!" She dug her keys out and jingled them. "And sometimes, my dear Rissa, you need a road trip." She picked up a brown sack by the kitchen island and hung it over her other wrist. "Let's go."

****

As road trips went, it was a long one. It gave Rissa time to study the world from a space place and inhale all the trashy snack food Barb picked up.

Rissa opened up another snack cake, this one chocolate with frosting, and bit into it. Flavor exploded on her tongue, and she sighed happily as she chewed.

Barb glanced over and chuckled. "Good thing Mandy passed out, or you wouldn't be all free and clear with that."

"Does she usually nap?" Rissa glanced in the back seat at Mandy in her booster chair. The girl, usually wired for sound, slept peacefully.

"For an hour or two." Barb fished out a snack and bit into it. "Then you'll wish she continued to do so." She looked in the rearview with a grin.

"Do all road trips come with this many snacks?" Rissa rooted around in the big brown bag for something else to put in her mouth. Another chocolate snack cake would fit the bill.

"Only the good ones." Barb washed her vanilla cake down with a cola.

"Noted." Rissa found her prize and opened it with a smug grin. Maybe road trips weren't so bad after all.

CHAPTER 26

Harmony Haven rested on five acres of manicured lawns. It housed fifteen residents with thirty staff. They offered twenty-four-hour care with home-cooked meals and customized meal plans, if necessary. Residents had private rooms and baths. There were three large common areas the residents could gather and plenty of natural light.

It was a single-story cheery red brick with a creamy yolk paint and blossoming hanging plants. The Haven, as everyone called it, resembled a Bed 'n' Breakfast more than an assisted-living community.

There were wide paved paths for walkers and wheelchairs. Each door outfitted with handicap buttons for easy opening. Benches dotted the lawn for rest or leisure. Residents could request a meal at one of the three picnic tables available.

Barb gave Rissa the overall description and fell silent. Mandy sat in the back seat, quiet at first. The closer they drove, the more restless she became.

"Mandy, love, play with your tablet. Put your headphones on."

"Yes, Mama!"

Rissa smiled at Mandy's eager tone. "She's been waiting for that."

"Of course she has." Barb rolled her eyes. "I wait until the last minute to offer it up. We're thirty minutes out, and she'll spend it blissed-out on alphabet songs and goofy characters she knows by heart." She paused. "It'll be a late drive back, but Mandy's doctors understand how important this is. I'll call a bit before we take her back, and they'll settle her in."

Rissa glanced over. "Does it bother you to visit her birth mother?"

"No. Not a bit." Barb sighed. "Mandy's mother has had a rough life. Someone attacked her with acid and left her blind and without use of her right hand. The acid splashed on her chest and has also limited her lung capacity."

"What the fuck is wrong with people?"

"I honestly don't know." Barb tapped her fingers on the steering wheel. "She was pregnant with Mandy when this happened. That's why Mandy has the issues she does."

"You said they let you adopt Mandy because they thought she was going to die?"

"Yes." Barb took a deep breath. "It was a closed adoption. I can understand why. But as Mandy grew up, she wanted to know. She persisted." Barb emphasized the word. "I contacted the agency, and they explained the situation. Then I explained it to Mandy."

She glanced at Rissa, and a tear rolled down her cheek. "Mandy said she needed to see if her Mama was okay. It didn't matter if her Mama couldn't see her. She would be a good person to her Mama because other people were mean, and she would show her nice."

"Fuck," Rissa muttered and glanced toward the back seat. "She's something, isn't she?"

"She's everything." Barb wiped her tears. "Mandy calls her mother 'Mom E' since her mother's name starts with an 'E', and it's adorable. El lets Mandy climb all over her and wheel her around. They giggle and share secrets. Mandy brushes her hair. They truly share a bond."

"Mom E!" Mandy repeated with a giggle. "I'm going to see 'Mom E'!" She wiggled in her seat and sang a song about the trip.

They arrived and parked twenty minutes later. Mandy took off her headphones and fumbled with her seatbelt. Barb gathered her things and helped the girl out.

Rissa hung back for a moment and studied the place with lethal precision. Doors. Roads. Staff. Everything catalogued and put in its place. She opened her car door, ducked her head, and followed the duo inside.

Rissa prepared for the harsh sting of bleach to her nostrils and found none. The living center smelled fresh with cleaning supplies and flowers placed every eight feet on tables and windows.

There was a low hum of music and voices that blended together as a nice melody. Staff wore soft scrubs and assisted guests with their needs. More than half the guests in wheelchairs with lack of mobility.

Barb escorted Mandy in, and Rissa warily followed. Rissa stepped completely inside and stopped.

The hair on the back of Rissa's neck stood straight up. Fight or flight came in strong, and she palmed the combat Troodon knife in her right jean pocket. One little flick, and her pointy friend would help clear a path.

Rissa walked slowly to the nearest wall and pressed her back against it. She kept Barb and Mandy in her sight as they talked to the receiving nurse to her right. Half the residents milled around in the largest common area with ambient music to her left.

At first, Rissa thought she dreamed. Real life didn't give you gifts such as this. She pricked her finger with her knife and acknowledged the pain. Maybe Karma did exist.

A nurse hovered close to the man dressed in royal blue pajamas in his wheelchair. Hands folded neatly in his lap. He stared out the farthest window, and Rissa could only stare at the profile he offered.

Rissa walked slowly toward the man. Her heart beat painfully in her chest. She caught her breath as she reached his left side. The room swam for a minute as she tried to focus her eyes on the resident.

"Hello, Miss." The blonde nurse smiled widely. "I'm Betty. This is Don. Did you want to visit with him?"

Rissa forced a smile as she looked down on Doc. She hadn't seen the white bib around his neck from her previous angle, nor the strap around his chest which allowed him to sit up straight. There were dry, white flakes around his mouth missed on clean-up and scruff on his cheeks and chin. "May I?"

"Oh, of course! Don doesn't usually have any visitors. Did you know him previously? He was a doctor, you know." Betty clicked her tongue against her teeth.

"Actually, I did." Rissa motioned to him. "What happened?"

"Stroke." Betty shook her head. "All that knowledge. Gone." She made a poofing motion with her hand. "Now he sits here and watches the birds." Betty smiled. "I'm going to go eat a yogurt on break. I'll be back in ten. Don't worry about Don. I fed him applesauce half an hour ago. He should be good. You'll be okay?" She already walked toward the front desk.

"Oh, we'll be fine!" Rissa waved her away with a smile. The smile dropped away as she wheeled Doc over to a bench and sat down.

Rissa curved her body into him so no one else could hear her. His weak and crooked body tried to pull away as best he could, but she would have none of that.

"You stay the fuck where you are, you worthless son of a bitch, or I'll come back in your dreams, and you'll think this is a picnic," Rissa warned.

Doc stilled immediately.

Rissa patted his leg. "You *can* teach an old doc new tricks." She looked into his eyes. "You're alive because I let you be. But you're also trapped every motherfucking day of your life. This is your lesson, you shitbag. Every day for the rest of your miserable life, Nurse Betty, over there, will spoon feed you and wipe your mouth. She'll strip you down and bathe you. She'll hold your dick to pee and wipe your ass."

Doc's hands moved and grabbed his pant legs. They pulled the fabric into small fists.

"You rode your power like a bolt of lightning. Striking everything in your path and not giving two fucks. You thought you were above recriminations. Above retaliations. No one could touch you."

Rissa fisted her right hand over his. "But I touched you, didn't I? You and every one of your fucking accomplices." She squeezed tighter. "People like me aren't disposable, Donnie. People like me are deadly. We're damaged. We're…difficult."

Doc made sounds in the back of his throat and tried to move his hands. Rissa tightened her grip. She felt his pinky stretch and let it go right before it broke.

Tears slid down Doc's face as he clutched his hands together.

"All your powerful alliances wrote you off, Donnie. You're useless. Nothing but defective grey matter in a rotting meat suit." Rissa cupped his chin and turned his face toward her. "But I won't ever forget you, Doc. Ever."

"Hello, you two! I'm back." Betty hurried over. "Have a good time catching up?" She bent down. "Oh. Don's been crying." She took some tissue from a pocket of her nurse's uniform and dabbed his eyes.

"We were talking about the good ol' days." Rissa stood. "They always get to him."

"You've been so kind to visit." Betty smiled. "I'm sure he appreciates it."

"Funny thing being, it was entirely a fluke." Rissa shook her head. "I'm here with friends visiting a relative. I guess I was meant to see Don today."

"That's crazy!" Betty grinned.

"Isn't it?" Rissa turned to walk off. "Have a good day!" She waved and went to find Barb and Mandy. They were nowhere in sight. The nurse at the front pointed Rissa to Room 12.

Rissa's emotions were in roller coaster mode. She knew she nearly reached maximum overdrive, but Mandy wanted her here, and how hard was it to meet her blind mother?

Rissa pushed the door open slowly and peeked inside. Mandy lay on the bed with her head on the woman's shoulder, and Barb sat in a chair in the far corner of the room on her phone.

An elderly black woman rocked back and forth in the far corner and knit a dark green and orange blanket. "I'm Nurse Verna. Don't ya mind me. Getting ready for a change of season."

"Wissa!" Mandy's head popped up, and she beamed. "Come meet my Mom E!" She stuck out her hand, and Rissa met it with her right.

Mandy pulled her closer and lay her head back down. Rissa stopped a couple feet away.

Mom E's right side of her face seemed to melt from forehead to neck. Her hairline started at her ear with wisps of grey and mottled red strands fell softly. She had no eyebrow or lashes and her eyelid fused permanently shut while the right side of her face drooped an inch lower than the other. Her mouth, surprisingly, nearly unharmed.

Mandy clung to a ravaged arm with deep furrows of damage, nearly to the bone in some areas, and a hand that now resembled a mash of bone and flesh. The acid took the tips of the fingers and fused the rest together in one clump like a dolphin's fin.

Rissa didn't feel pity for the woman, but empathy. For the first time, she saw another being who had been damaged beyond repair. She wanted to ask what it felt like. Did she hate as darkly as Rissa?

Barb looked up from her phone. "You're right on time. We've about fifteen minutes before El takes her nap and then lunch."

"Wissa! Go on the other side!"

Rissa walked to the foot of the bed and glanced up at the patient. The right side took the greatest concentration of the acid. Mom E showed dots on the left side of her face from splatter, but nothing so fierce as to melt her face onto her facial bones. She missed a small piece of her nose and another of her left ear. Yet, her arm appeared undamaged. Mom E kept her eyes closed but smiled as she listened to Mandy boss Rissa around.

"My darling is a bossy darling, isn't she?" Mom E rasped.

Barb laughed. "She takes after you."

"True." Mom E chuckled and then gasped.

The black woman in the corner stood up. "Calm yourself, El. I don't want to have to hook you up to the oxygen machine." She patted the patient. "Softly, child. Softly." She rearranged the covers. "Now. Eye drop real quick. Then I'll leave you alone until lunch." She paused. "Maybe."

Mom E opened her left eye, and Rissa's world stood still.

CHAPTER 27

Sometimes, when Doc beat her, Rissa forgot to breathe. When the blows hurt so bad, she couldn't conceive of breathing air into fragile body because it would only hurt worse. Most times she would faint from the pain and lack of oxygen.

This hurt a thousand times worse.

But Rissa, the devil bless her, didn't flinch. "I'm Rissa. Would you like me to call you El?"

"Please," she whispered and extended her left hand to shake.

Rissa glanced down at the offering and bit her tongue so hard it bled. She slid her hand briefly into the older woman's and back out in the blink of an eye.

Verna sat back down with a nod. "New friends are butterfly blessings. Always come and land when you least expect it." She smiled up at Rissa. "Miss Mandy is the biggest blessing of them all."

"Yes, she is." El reached over and squeezed Mandy with her left arm. "Thank you for coming to see me."

"I love you, Mom E." Mandy scooted up and kissed El's cheek. She clung to the woman's body with a tight hug.

"You and El talk for a little bit longer." Barb checked her phone. "I have to make a call, but I'll be right back." She smiled and waved as she walked out the door.

Rissa followed her.

Barb looked behind her and frowned. "Everything okay?"

"Sure. Think I'll step outside for some air." Rissa nodded and beelined for the front doors. She hit them at an accelerated pace and briefly thought about running until she collapsed. Anything to get this weight off of her. Rissa fought to breathe as the bulk settled in her chest.

The deformed woman in that bed was her mother. The truth feather landed on the elephant sitting on her chest, and her breath hitched. Too much weight.

Rissa's vision narrowed, and she sank onto a wooden bench with her head loose on her shoulders. She broke out in a sweat, and every sound dimmed until the only thing she felt and heard was the crazy beat of her desperate heart.

She pressed her hand to her chest, and made a face as the pain radiated through her. Rissa would die here. Die in the place where her life-giver withered, and her soul-taker slept. Maybe this was the justice of which people spoke. Her chest tightened again, and Rissa clenched her jaw and sat with the pain. She wouldn't cheapen the ride.

****

Rissa squinted in the dim light. Her chest no longer felt like someone breaking free from her ribcage from the inside. Her heart beat normally. She frowned.

"What in the fuck were you doing?" Barb hissed at her and smacked her foot under the cover.

"What?" Rissa sat up in the small bed and looked around. Her head immediately revolted. She clasped her temples. "Lower your fucking voice," she pleaded.

"Lower my voice?" Barb whispered and narrowed her eyes. "I'm goddamn whispering right now, you fucking idiot!"

"Where am I?" Rissa frowned.

"We're still in the care facility, you absolute...maniac!" Barb glared.

"Okay." Rissa held up her hand. "One, I need something for this bitchin' headache. Two, why am I a maniac?"

"Jesus Christ, Rissa! You scared the hell out of me. I look out the window after my phone call." Barb points at a wall. "You're fucking clutching your chest on a goddamn bench, and then you fall out of it like a bug that's been sprayed."

Rissa blinked. "Oh. I'm not dying?"

Barb's lips flattened into a thin line. She shrugged. "Oh? Not dying today?" She slapped Rissa's feet three more times. "No, you fucking idiot, you had a major anxiety attack. Your heart rate was a hundred and seventy-two. Your blood pressure went through the fucking roof."

Rissa sat back. "Oh."

"The fact I'm glad you're alive eclipses the fact I'd like to beat you to death for being so nonchalant." Barb sank down at the foot of the bed. "They put you in a small room to recover. Mandy's still with El. It's a little after three." She blew out an unsteady breath. "What's up?"

Rissa's head snapped.

"Oh. You think I don't notice things?" Barb rolled her eyes. "Listen, kid. I notice. I noticed you spoke with an old friend earlier. Funny how the world works. I noticed you didn't want to touch El which I thought maybe because you don't like to touch people in general, but now I wonder if there's a different reason. As for the bench..." Barb glared. "You were in pain but did nothing about it, and these questions you continue to ask, seem to me like you thought you were dying and were totally on board with that bullshit."

Rissa thought hard about snapping right back, but she didn't have the energy. "Thought I had a heart attack, and I wasn't opposed." She pulled her feet up. "Don't even fucking think about it."

Barb put her hands in her lap and looked at Rissa. "I watched them check your vitals, and I saw the looks in their eyes when they saw your scars on your arms and wrists. One nurse said a rosary. When they realized it was only an anxiety attack, they looked to me for answers about the scars."

Rissa's fun-time day overflowed. If exactly one more thing happened, she'd slit her wrists and happily call it a life. She sighed and looked at Barb.

"I told them you'd been kidnapped and tortured."

Rissa stared.

"I told them you'd lived through hell, but sometimes pieces of it cropped up, and you never knew when. I told them I was your nurse, and I helped as best I could, but you're the fighter."

"You told them?" Rissa swallowed hard. They may have seen her scars, but Barb shared her wounds.

Barb nodded. "And all these professionals looked at you with admiration, Rissa. Because you survived."

"Instead of being some junkie from the streets?" Rissa's eyes cut through her. She hated they saw her scars. Hated being weak. She would rather have died on the fucking bench than pitied on some stretcher. "I don't need their sympathy."

"Rissa," Barb began.

"Save it." Rissa shook her head. "They know the 'Once Upon a Time' part, but do they know the rest? Did you tell them I could creep around in their head and really fuck up their lives? I could make them do shit that would make sadists throw up? I could make them kill others? I could pull their sickest fantasy from their mind and make it real?!?"

"Why always the dark?"

Rissa thought it a fair question and didn't flinch. "Because Barb. I'm comfortable in the dark. In the hallways of your mind, the dark knows the secrets. The dark shines brightly on every nightmare proud as a silver dollar. The dark sinks its sharp teeth into you the moment you turn your back. The dark inhibits, but what if you've the key?"

"The teeth of the gold to unlock the menagerie of bad dreams and hallucinations and sinister laughs and gasping pains. Sharp knives on bare flesh. Hooks to move wiggling bodies. And the screams? The screams of the senseless and insane as they wail for mercy, and there is none to be dealt!" Rissa clawed her throat and gasped for air as Barb brought her forward and thumped her on the back to clear her airway.

Rissa finally inhaled. She reached out and clamped her left hand around Barb's right arm. Cheeks puffed in and out as she tried to even out her breath. And glacier blue eyes faded back to the light green they knew.

"Barb," Rissa rasped. "Something visited. Something near." She growled low. "I don't like surprises, and I don't like going to parties uninvited."

"Your eyes." Barb motioned. "They were ice-blue."

"It was asleep. Whether male or female, I couldn't tell, but it enjoyed the visit. I'm tired enough to allow it. No defenses to speak of and pissed off enough not to pay attention. I'll make sure it doesn't happen again."

"What does it want?"

Rissa smiled. "It wants to play. Strong one wins. Weak one dies. Eventually." She looked at Barb. "Ready everyone to leave. I need to go home and prepare. That was the invitation. Now? I need to craft my acceptance."

She swung her legs over the side of the bed with a great deal more energy and slid her shoes on. Rissa nearly let the shock and fury override her common sense. She paused. Wintry blue eyes?

Rissa opened the door and walked down the hall to the large

common area. No Doc. She saw Nurse Betty and flagged her down.

Betty spoke first. "I hoped you were still here." She put her hands in her front pockets and appeared upset. "Don had an episode."

"An episode?" Rissa's wheels turned. "A bad one?"

Betty nodded. "I'm so sorry. It came out of nowhere. Another stroke." Betty blinked to hold back tears. "They took him to the hospital, but they don't know if he'll make it. Even if he does, he'll go on hospice."

It would be poor form for Rissa to smile. She bit the inside of her lip and simply nodded. She'd been wrong. Doc had been useful one last time. Those fuckers booby-trapped him and waited to see if she would ever arrive and take the bait.

There were no accidents.

CHAPTER 28

Rissa asked Barb to drop her off half an hour's walk from her cabin. She needed time to think and plan. New variables crowded her brain, and it was a quick shuffle before she dealt herself into a new and deadly game.

Barb looked worried, but Rissa didn't have the time to try and placate her. Rissa mistakenly thought she'd beat the system, except the system worked as the undead. You could knock the living shit out of it, and it still kept coming.

She checked with Kase. All technology scrubbed. He'd been succinct and delighted. Years of records wiped. The three additional facilities in Oklahoma shuttered with nine other children freed and being cared for in the catacombs.

Rissa wanted to ask but didn't trust herself right now. The less information she had, the better. The nine weighed on her mind, but she focused on the issue at hand. Someone powerful wanted to play for all the marbles. Their mind. Her mind. If she lost, they would have her. They would begin again. And Rissa would be in no shape to fight anyone.

The risk.

Rissa walked up the steep drive to her cabin and dissected her thoughts. She didn't pretend her loss would be trivial. Her loss translated into thousands of more deaths for unknowns. Whether she was conscious or not at that point, she would become, again, the fucking weapon.

She didn't hold out any hope she would be spared the indignity of being a vegetable with incredible brain capabilities. The moment Rissa lost, there would be no more meals or showers. No more meds or half-assed attempts at conversation.

They'd kill her body and harvest her brain power. If they couldn't do that, they'd simply pull the sheet over her head and call it a day.

Rissa made peace with it as she trudged the last few steps to her cabin. She unlocked her home and unarmed her alarm. Locked the door. Set the alarm.

She firmly pushed Barb, Mandy, and her mother into a small room and sealed the door tight. Rissa blocked it with the last ounce of caring she possessed in her being. When the door faded into the walls of her mind, she turned and planned.

****

First item belonged to Doc Donnie. Rissa made herself comfortable on the couch and dozed off. She walked down the corridors of her mind until she reached his access point.

The shattered remains of a bomb scattered outside his door. Clever, Rissa admitted. Probably triggered by his vitals going haywire. The bomb transferred to her as soon as she reached a certain unconscious state and detonated. The blowback took Doc back to stroke world with the knowledge he wouldn't survive it. Neat trick.

Rissa opened the door and walked inside.

Doc lay lifeless in his hospital bed. No machines here. No incessant beeping to remind the living the patient still had a heartbeat. Simply one sorry bastard who stole her life and now had an idea his was about to go the same route.

"Don't be smug."

Rissa flinched at the sound of his voice. She looked up to see he watched her from the opposite corner. He wore the same pajamas he had on at their first meeting at his house.

"Dead man talking."

"Seemingly." Doc looked down at his body in irritation. "There wasn't any need to go this far. I would have gladly done anything to hurt you."

"And have." Rissa studied him. "Yet, here you are. Looking like a salmon who's had a bad day." She paused. "You're as much a pawn as I was."

"Hoping to regain some type of upper hand, Red?" Doc shrugged. "You won't. I marked you for life, child." He grinned at her in triumph. "I owned you every second you were on that hospital bed. You killed for me, and I took from you." Doc held up his hand and ticked off his fingers. "Your family. Your ability to have children. Your childhood. Your innocence. Your fucking humanity."

Rissa smiled as Doc's fingers bent completely back and broke at the first knuckle. He screamed and turned white as a sheet and sank to the floor holding his wounded hand.

She stooped down and winked. "Maybe, Doc. But you're not quite dead. And goddamn it, I bet right about now you wish I had some humanity." Rissa broke both his ankles with a thought.

Doc tried to slither back to the wall and out of sight. Rissa stood and looked at the body on the bed and then glanced at the moaning man on the floor.

"Karma's a bitch, you fucker, and so am I." She studied him. "There's still a bit of fun to be had."

****

Rissa left Doc in a pile of pain subconsciously while he coded at the hospital. No more dirty bombs by the sadistic doctor. Good on that.

She woke and stretched. It would soon be dark, and she needed her wits about her. Rissa made a thick turkey sandwich and took it back to the couch. She sipped her water, and let her mind wander. A forest walk sounded perfect this evening.

There were too many loose strings in her life, but she pushed them all away to ready herself. Rissa did not want to play this evening. She wanted to prepare herself completely because it would take her entire being for this game.

Doc's words replayed in her head. He did, indeed, take those things from her. He did so gleefully, but he also did so on orders. While the messenger enjoyed the delivery, the real criminal in the proceedings issued the orders. If Doc were a demon, then Satan, himself, waited for her.

But she survived those years in hell. Over half her life at the whims and orders of the merciless and sadistic.

What did that make her? A pawn, surely. But also, a player. Her watchers never saw what she saw. Never felt what she felt. All they could do was observe from afar.

Each experience, every experience, shaped her and her alone.

****

Rissa only thought she danced with the devil before. Now they were due for a real meeting of the minds. Winner kills all.

She prepared as best she could. The invitation, a pulsing red sign, that simply read, "to begin."

Rissa skirted the sign for three days before she reached out and touched the summons. She protected herself as best she could. The sign could be a trigger set to explode her brain to bits, but Rissa doubted the mastermind behind her fucked-up life wanted her dead.

No. He wanted to play. And win.

Rissa fell through six feet of air before she landed on her feet. The room lit like a stadium at game time. But each corner an endless shadow.

"You are?"

"You can call me Paul, though you really need to call me 'master'."

Rissa silently stared in his direction.

"You fascinated me from the beginning, child." The young man stepped from the dark with a devil's grin. He wore khakis and a light blue polo. Face chiseled by wealth and a persistent plastic surgeon's tool. Teeth blinding in the overwhelming light of the room. Pale blue eyes, cold as ice, studied her. "How could I use you?"

"You didn't want to know how I became a dream walker?" Rissa asked. "Didn't want to create an army?"

"I only needed one." He paused. "One who would do exactly as I ordered." Bright teeth flashed. "And, you were such a delight!" He clapped his hands together, and they echoed in the large space. "Doctor Hamilton offered you up at such a good price that we jumped on it." Paul chuckled. "Then you offed the good doc, and we *really* got a bargain!"

"Glad that worked out for you."

"Oh, child. We were doing fine until you thought other people mattered." Paul rolled his eyes. "Even worse when you thought you mattered." He brushed his right hand through the air. "I didn't buy you for your ego or thoughts. I needed obedience."

"I don't bark, fucker." Rissa glared at him.

Paul's head snapped around, and he pinned her with his eyes. "Oh, you did, bitch. You so did. For years. You barked on command. Woof, woof, weapon. Woof, woof." He aimed his right hand at her. "See, you don't have the option to have an opinion. I bought those right the fuck out of you."

"Did you, Paul?" Rissa pushed away from the wall. "You wanted my hate. You wanted their pain through me. You wanted death and destruction." She smiled sweetly. "I was more than a dream walker. I was your wet dream."

"You're sick," he growled.

"*I'm* sick?"

"You owe me everything!" Paul shouted. "You have no family. Your father sold you to Doctor Hamilton. You were a menace to your class in school at such a young age. People like you need to be kept separate and utilized. You're not built for this world. I *saved* you."

"From what?" Rissa demanded. Sparks flew from her fingers as she approached the man who stole her life and so many others. "What did you save me from, you heartless motherfucker?"

Paul's grin broadened until it was almost obscene. "Yourself."

CHAPTER 29

Rissa threw out her hands, but her nemesis disappeared in a wink. She knew the sneaky asshole would try and finish her when she least expected it. She needed her guard up with heightened senses ready.

Paul disappeared from their meeting room, but now he wandered out there in the dark. His best chance would be a sneak attack. But he also may have set up traps along the way.

Rissa focused herself. She would not lose this game, no matter the cost. She opened the door and stepped into the dark.

A red button flashed in front of her, and Rissa pressed it.

Lights came on in groups, and she cursed under her breath. That piece of shit made his headquarters their game board. She appeared to be on the executive floor of the building. Lush crimson carpet and dark wood walls. Haughty paintings of men with pointed chins and icy eyes. Obviously, ancestors of her latest nightmare. Glass doors that led into break rooms, meeting rooms, and offices. Rissa took nothing at face value.

Vision, in dreams, was as useless as sunglasses at midnight.

Rissa wore black jeans and a black tank top. Black leather boots and a small ponytail. She walked silently but knew he watched her. Rissa felt him as a mouse could feel a cat nearby.

A man from the nearest portrait leapt from it and tackled Rissa to the ground, he slashed at her face with a knife, but she held up her arm to block him. He cut the outside of her left arm below the elbow, but she incinerated him with her right hand and stood up.

Rissa set the other portraits on fire and watched them burn. Didn't mean they wouldn't be back. Only meant she may have a bigger preparation time.

She materialized a Fairbairn-Sykes fighting knife in her right hand and allowed the slight weight to settle her. Rissa could change it to literally anything, but she loved this knife. After her incarceration, she developed an affinity for blades.

Rissa stopped the bleeding on her arm and cocked her head to the side. A small noise in one of the rooms ahead signaled more cool games and opportunities to bleed. This carnival was some serious bullshit.

The glass shattered, and Rissa shielded her eyes and took a step back. Doc Hamilton stumbled through the door. He'd been slit from throat to ankle on both sides. His skin fluttered like a tent flap in a blizzard while his muscles hung ragged on white bone. Brain matter oozed from a cracked cranium and all former facial features slid happily down the front of his skull.

"Rissa," he lisped and reached out. "Come here, child. Come to me." He wiped his mouth, and his lips slid to the floor. "You've been a bad girl."

Rissa squared her jaw. "Go back to hell, Doc." She threw fire with her left hand and watched Doc Hamilton's corpse burn, except for his skeleton.

The fire died out, and the skeleton still stood. "You've always been bad, child." The skeleton reached out again, and Rissa swung a sledgehammer at the already-cracked skull. It shattered into a dozen pieces, and the entire skeleton disappeared.

"You always have someone else do your dirty work, don't you?" Rissa yelled down the hall. "Not only useless, but a fucking coward."

He may, or may not, have sent the great white sharks at her words. Okay. He did.

One second, Rissa played piñata with an old doctor, the next second, she met dozens of hungry sharks, green eyes to obsidian ones.

Rissa quickly enclosed herself in a protective bubble in the middle of the hallway. Soft crimson carpet beneath her feet while many predators with rows and rows of serrated teeth swam by.

These sharks weren't lengthy per se, no longer than a yard at the max, but they displayed vicious characteristics such as biting each other and gnawing at the tube Rissa stood. Blood filled the hallway.

And in each of their dead eyes, Rissa knew Paul watched. She summoned the creature from his mind, from the minds of the sharks.

They called it Orca.

It came from the opposite direction. Massive creature of black and white. Smooth like a bullet. It swam faster and faster.

Suddenly, the sharks sensed its presence and attempted to hide against the walls, but it was no use.

The orca opened its mouth wide. Rissa saw its huge pink tongue, and the teeth that lined its mouth. It turned to its left side and took half the sharks in one bite with a flip of its tale.

She saw the water fill with scarlet and the fin of a shark float by. Rissa swallowed hard and waited. The orca made a lap and returned to flip on its right side. The sharks never stood a chance.

The orca bumped its big head against Rissa's tube. She smiled and patted the smooth leathery skin. It disappeared the next moment.

Rissa debated her next move. Surely Paul could see she had counter-maneuvers? Couldn't he? The door between their minds open on both sides. Limited views but enough for counter-measures.

Did Paul forget she dealt in nightmares? Hideous creatures and depraved depths of people brought to life? He could throw deadly creatures at her all day, and she would respond. But none of it touched her. Because thanks to him and his ilk, she couldn't be touched.

Perhaps, he finally realized it, too.

Rissa continued her walk down the crimson hall. She paused at clear doors and peered inside. No Paul. She resumed her pace and stepped into the circle. Rissa felt the rope tighten around her ankle.

Swift. Painful.

The jerk of it snapped Rissa's neck back, and she clawed the air searching for something to grab and stabilize her. No such thing existed. The air popped as she disappeared.

****

"I've always wanted to see this up close and personal." The words echoed throughout the room.

Rissa blinked and tried to establish her bearings. She could only see the ceiling.

No.

NO.

Rissa struggled to move but found her arms and legs bound. Bile rushed into her throat, and she choked it back while she fought for composure. "Why does everyone want me back in this goddamn bed?" she screamed.

"I've seen tapes, of course. But to have you here? At my bidding? Helpless?" Paul paused. "Your time at the facility will seem like an absolute party in comparison." Paul smirked. "Do you even understand why we made you kill certain people? Or is that beyond your simple brain?"

Rissa heard footsteps approach and stiffened. The ball was in a mad man's court.

Paul loomed over her with a devil's grin and gleaming eye. "Look at our little Rissa. Right back where she started." He chuckled. "I didn't know how much I'd enjoy seeing this." Paul narrowed his eyes and studied her. "Important people aren't important. They are merely totems which can be changed at will. We don't want to kill presidents, queens, or kings. They're simply pawns. Give them some power, and they think they're running the show. When we're done with them, we bury them in the dirt like cat shit and move on. Important people only have egos we've given them.

Power comes from underneath. Below these so-called 'important' people are those who create worlds. They shape the dialogue. They push the rhetoric. They kill the worthy and push the puppets to the top. Straighten the strings. Burn the hopes and dreams of the people." Paul smiled. "You are the homicidal key, bitch."

Rissa set her jaw and forced herself to meet his eyes. She could see the spittle on the side of his mouth. The stubble above his lip. Pure insanity danced in his pale blue eyes.

"What? No cocky words? Bullshit threats?" He leaned farther down. "Talk of tearing me apart?" Paul laughed in her face. He stopped abruptly and grabbed her chin. "Listen to me, you little shit. You. Are. Nothing." Paul let her go and stepped back. "Except for my little experiment."

"What are you talking about?"

"You really are simple, aren't you?" Paul rolled his eyes. "You're mine. Again. Mentally." He smiled and slapped her hard enough she bit her tongue. "I will extract your physical location, and our relationship will continue again."

Rissa swallowed blood and glared up at him. "Go fuck yourself, little man."

"Ah, there you are." Paul sighed. "Nearly thought this would be no fun at all." He smiled and leaned down. "I'm going to hurt you in ways you never dreamed." Paul clapped his hand over his mouth and giggled.

The mad man leaned back and stretched. "Should I start with your fingers or toes?" He frowned. "Ears? Eyes?" He cocked his head to the side. "Sodomy or gang rape?" Paul considered the options.

"Not man enough to do it yourself?" Rissa glared up at him.

"I didn't know you cared." Paul looked her over. "It would be like fucking a boy." He made a face. "Not my first choice." He shrugged. "Not my last." Paul reached down to undo her pants.

Rissa grabbed his hand.

The look of surprise on this man's face nearly made letting herself be caught and bound worth it.

"Let me go!" Paul struggled to disengage, but Rissa held tight.

In the blink of an eye, Paul lay strapped to the table, and Rissa looked down at him. She smiled.

"Rissa. Let me go. We can work this out. Nothing personal." Paul looked up at her with a small confident smile.

She patted his arm. "Oh, Paul. It's all personal, you sick fuck."

His smile faded, and he struggled against the constraints.

"Keep it up. Let's see if you give yourself some cool scars like I have." Rissa pulled up her shirt sleeve and showed those at her wrist. "Or maybe I can spend all fucking night shoving your ass full of needles, and you can have an arm that looks like this." She pulled her sleeve up farther.

"I didn't tell them to do that! They decided it on site. Doctor Fullbright said they used it to control you." Icy blue eyes stared into hers.

"How's that going?" Rissa shook her head. "Did you think you stood a shot against me?" She casually reached down and broke Paul's nose. Blood gushed out.

"I had you!" he screamed.

"You had what I gave you, you motherfucker!" Rissa freed him and plastered him against the far wall. "You are no match for me!" Sparks flew from her fingers as she approached him. "I am death. I am the scream in the silence. I am the fear in your bones. The nightmare that haunts you."

"You can't kill me. I made you. You can go. Live whatever is left of a life for you. I will leave you alone."

"Leave me alone?" Rissa growled low. "You wouldn't know how, you piece of shit." She bared her teeth. "You've been in my territory for two days now. Asleep. Unaware. I thumbed through your head like a goddamn catalog. I've been burning your life all fucking day, and you haven't noticed a thing."

CHAPTER 30

Paul frowned. "That's impossible." He wiped his nose and shook his head. "No one can do that. No. I went to work today." He glared at her. "I went to work today!"

"You're asleep in the safe room in your office. Your wonderful secretary, Betty, gave you a bit of drugged tea the other day. She's another piece of work, isn't she? Helps you find children. Pays off parents or helps rid the world of them." Rissa brought the woman's body to Paul with a thought. She'd been drugged as well. Permanently.

Paul looked at the body and then at Rissa. "What else have you done?"

Rissa held up her hand and ticked off her fingers. "Let's see. Killed her. Am killing you. Shut down Sunmos Labs completely. Will burn your offices to the ground. Disappear." She smiled sweetly.

"Someone like you can't hide." Paul sneered. "It's impossible. Look at your ego." He tried to step forward but still couldn't move from the wall. "You think our people won't find you? Take you? Kill you?" He rolled his eyes. "Stupid bitch."

"I like my odds better than yours." Rissa stepped close to him and pressed her sizzling right hand against his chest.

Paul jerked and groaned as 100v moved through his body. Rissa controlled the current to cause pain but not to stop his heart, if he had one.

The current burned through his shirt and singed his chest hairs. He also had a lovely brand in the shape of her handprint.

Rissa pulled her knife out and studied its sharp edges. Weapons never failed you. You failed the weapon.

"I planned on cutting you into tiny pieces, Paul. Scattering bits of you about and listening to your cries of pain like the most beautiful opera. You know. I like opera." Rissa tilted her head to the side. "Surprised me, too. Still finding out about myself."

Paul's icy blue eyes studied her, but he said nothing. The breath whistled in and out his lungs. The blood from his nose now a mere trickle. The smell of burnt flesh rose from his chest.

"I've thought about and tossed out at least five or six dozen scenarios of your demise." Rissa met his eyes. "None seemed to fit the bill, and, I can tell you, I didn't care for it a bit. Because you, Paul, you are special."

"Cut the bullshit," he snarled. "Fucking kill me and know the hell you unleashed."

"But then, it came to me." Rissa held the knife up. "Scars are stories, whether we like the tales or not. And Paul, I want you to tell my account. No cheating." She smiled and put the knife in her left hand. "Oh! And I'm ambidextrous." The rest of his shirt disintegrated with a thought.

Rissa mentally closed Paul's mouth and buried her knife a good three inches below his right collarbone. He spasmed against the wall and made incomprehensible noises.

She withdrew it a bit and proceeded to make the first letter of her name in capital form. The "R" looked nice against Paul's clammy skin, and the blood slid as tears. Rissa kept him from passing out. It was the least she could do.

"Stay with me Paul. Aren't you glad my name isn't longer?" Rissa planted her knife back in his skin for the "i" and dug deep for the straight line. She worked the weapon back and forth into his skin for the dot on top. Marvelous.

Her nemesis seemed a bit pale now. Perhaps the blood from his nose and the letter leakage caught up with him.

"Hey, hey asshole! I'm not even close to finished!" Rissa tweaked Paul's nose.

He pulled his head back so fast it banged against the wall, and his eyes watered more.

"The next two letters require a bit more real estate." Rissa eyed the pale man's stomach with a disgusted look. "I'd hate to have to go below the waist, but I may."

She thought Paul's eyes were insane before. Now they were rolling in his head like a crazed animal. Rissa lifted the gag from his mouth.

"Thoughts?"

"Please," he wheezed. "Don't."

Rissa muted him again. She would sooner wake him up, give him directions to her cabin, and invite him for a picnic lunch than go anywhere near his genitals. But he didn't need to know that.

She hummed as she worked. They'd robbed her of music. *Music.* Rissa could barely fathom. There were billions of songs on this earth she'd never heard. If she were not quiet, she listened to the rhythm of the world.

Rissa shielded her hand as she worked on the last letter. Blood poured from Paul's wounds, and he looked as white as the wall he was pinned. Every once in a bit, she would press her fingers into his wound to make sure he stayed conscious.

Rissa finished and stood up. She buried her knife, up to the hilt, in Paul's thigh. "Your story closes soon, Paul. Your life seeps out of you drip by drip. Everything you dreamed destroyed by me." She grabbed his chin and made him look at her. "I made you. I marked you. I finished you, you motherfucker. Take that knowledge to your grave." Rissa shoved his head back against the wall. It hit and then lolled forward, useless, on his shoulders.

She heard his heartbeat slow and pushed.

In real time, a dying Mr. Paul Shelton pressed a red button in his safe room which triggered explosives on each of the three floors of his building. The only casualties on every floor included his secretary and those who worked for Sunmos Corporation as special contractors. These special contractors acquired and disposed of assets for Mr. Shelton.

The devil, himself, marked with careful precision by the girl who escaped. Truly sad no one would ever admire her artwork.

Rissa heard the last beat of Paul's miserable heart and disappeared.

CHAPTER 31

Rissa woke on her couch with dry mouth, hollow stomach, and the fierce need to go to the bathroom. She hopped up to empty her bladder and washed her hands.

She made a roast beef sandwich, thought better of it, and made two. Filled up the biggest plastic cup she had with ice water, drained it, and filled it again.

Her equilibrium and sight wavered between normal and not really. Rissa felt her way around the cabin until she made her way back to the couch with food and drink.

It had been the longest dream walk she'd ever taken.

Rissa inhaled one sandwich, told herself to breathe, and slowed down for the second. She still felt like she walked the high wire with no net. The longer she spent awake, the more she hoped that feeling went away.

There were no rules for what she'd done. Spending so long in the dark didn't bode well, but she would do it again. If she left one thread for anyone to pull, she may as well be dead.

Rissa drank some more water and took two pills for the massive headache which only started as soon as she opened her eyes. She would check and see Sunmos Corporation went up in smoke, literally.

It would wait until tomorrow.

She fought to keep her eyes open and berated herself for not thinking this far ahead. Rissa used all her adrenaline. Her entire battery. She would be helpless now. At least until she received enough rest and sustenance to help her body.

The paper plate slid to the floor, and the empty plastic cup fell to the floor and bounced a couple times before it stilled.

Rissa slept.

****

"Wissa! Watch me!" Mandy ran around her front yard with blonde hair flying. Her butterfly dress, with sewn-on translucent wings, sparkled in the afternoon sun.

Barb grilled lunch in the back while Rissa watched the energetic eleven-year-old zip around the trees. She still hadn't told either female that Mandy was her sister. Some things were too good to spoil.

"You're way too fast!" Rissa smiled. "With all that energy. Probably those gorgeous wings."

Mandy stopped and turned her head to admire the colors.

Rissa opened her mouth to say something when she saw the dart puncture the wing. She ran toward Mandy.

The next dart hit the little girl in the neck, and she turned to Rissa with a look of fear and surprise. Her pupils shrank to almost nothing, and she fell to the grass.

There were six armed fighters dressed head-to-toe in black military grade uniforms and weapons. Five marched toward Rissa while the sixth scooped Mandy up as if she weighed nothing.

Two split from the five and walked around the back. Two shots fired, and Rissa swallowed her scream.

Three fighters stopped six feet in front of her.

"The girl is ours. The mother is dead. Come with us, or die right now."

Rissa looked at Mandy's lifeless body and swallowed. "I'll come."

The first soldier raised their rifle and...

...Rissa woke up to a scream.

It echoed through the cabin, and she didn't understand why it didn't stop until she realized she was the one screaming.

Rissa's body trembled, and she wrapped her arms around herself. What if they knew? She grabbed her phone and looked up Sunmos Corporation with shaking hands.

Ashes.

No more. No more. No more. Rissa repeated the words in her head until she stopped trembling. They would never come for Mandy because Rissa either killed or erased them.

Rissa took deep breaths in her nose and exhaled through her mouth. She knew better than to expect the nightmares to disappear. She also realized when her defenses were down, she was at the mercy of every dark thing in her mind. There were masses.

She would try to rest more today and seek out Barb tomorrow. Rissa needed to clear things up, but she needed to visit Elizabeth first.

****

Rissa took a car to the bus station and a bus until she had to take another car. She arrived at Haven House a little after one o'clock, determined to finally learn about her fractured past.

She had seen the worst of people. The depths of their depravity. The sins of their souls. Rissa enacted the bidding of bastards. She had *been* the worst of people.

Rissa checked in and walked slowly to Elizabeth's room. She finished lunch twenty minutes earlier and now rested comfortably in her room. As comfortably as one could be with an acid-washed body and complete blindness.

Rissa turned the knob and pushed the door open quietly and

peered inside. Verna, her nurse, absent.

Elizabeth turned her head slightly. "Who is it?"

"It's Rissa." She cleared her throat slightly. "Um, sorry to interrupt. I only wanted to stop by and check on you."

"You came by before with Mandy?"

"Yes, but only me today." Rissa shut the door behind her and moved closer to the bed.

"I appreciate you checking on me." Elizabeth smoothed down the blanket over her lap. "I rarely have visitors." Her hands stopped. "They said you fell ill. Are you okay?" She turned her head in Rissa's direction.

"Never better." Rissa proceeded to the side of the bed. "Thank you for asking." She looked down at her mother and didn't know what to feel.

They both bore scars as testament to a wretched life. Did Elizabeth still think about her dream walker daughter? Was this the price she paid for her?

"Is Mandy your only child?"

"Yes." Elizabeth smiled. It faded a bit. "They tell me she is."

Rissa took Elizabeth's right hand in both of hers. "What do you mean?"

"I thought...I thought I had another daughter." Elizabeth's soft voice drifted off. "I think I was confused." She frowned. It pulled her scars together, and she winced. "I was pregnant with Mandy. I must have been thinking about her. It's a miracle she survived."

"It is," Rissa agreed. She studied the woman in the bed. Fading red hair. Scarred beyond recognition to those who knew her. A figure she, her daughter, barely remembered between traumas.

Verna walked through the door and smiled at the pair. "Does my heart good to see my girl with visitors. Been with this child since the beginning." She hustled over and grabbed a dark green crochet blanket in-progress. "You two keep visiting. I'll be out in the commons." She waved as she shut the door behind her.

"I wouldn't have made it without her." Elizabeth sighed. "I think she willed me to live, in the beginning. I only remember the pain."

Rissa squeezed her hand gently. "Do you dream?"

"Dream?" She frowned. "A little. Why do you ask?"

"I know this sounds odd, but please, humor me. I could use an afternoon nap, and you look a bit tired. I'd love to hear what you dream about. Do you think it's possible to nod off?" Rissa held her breath.

Elizabeth smiled. "I didn't want to rush you out, but I nap more than I'm awake most days. I'd love to sleep a bit. I'll have a bit more energy to chat."

"Wonderful." Rissa exhaled. She fought the fear in her chest. Worst case? Elizabeth wouldn't remember her. Would likely shun her. Wouldn't be the cruelest thing to happen to Rissa, but damn close. She kept Elizabeth's hand in hers and closed her eyes.

CHAPTER 32

Rissa stood in a long dark hallway lit by a single yellow overhead bulb. Various colors of doors speckled the walls both left and right. Some with windows and door knobs. A few flashed different jewel colors as kaleidoscope lightning.

Elizabeth's mind shuttered like an old home forgotten when its occupants passed away and no one bothered to check on it. Did the accident push her memories away, or did somebody do it on purpose?

Rissa slowly brought both hands up and illuminated the length of the hall with soft white light. A moment of silence before a lost woman's voice echoed.

"Who's there?"

Rissa knew, better than anybody, how it felt to be wandering around in the dark with no anchor. "It's Rissa. I'm coming toward you. Don't be frightened." *I'm only a serial killer, but also your daughter, and I don't know which I'm more scared to tell you.*

A part of Rissa wanted to peek into some of the rooms she passed, but she continued down the hall and toward her mother. Rissa didn't know if blind people could see in dreams. If it mattered if they were blinded later in life. She didn't know if she was about to put her mother in a catatonic state by imparting some traumatic facts about her guest.

"Rissa? Are you almost here?"

"Almost." Rissa waved her hand and brought herself to the end of the hallway. She couldn't take any more suspense. What would be, would be.

A hand reached from the shadows.

Rissa gently took it and pulled her mother into the light.

Shock rooted Rissa to the floor. This was Elizabeth Clay of old. Scarlett tresses and pale green eyes. Ivory skin and an old dark blue robe wrapped around her slight form. Her mind clung to the vision it remembered last.

"Can you see?" Rissa looked into her eyes but saw no recognition.

"I cannot." Elizabeth shook her head. "At times, I think I have dreamt and saw, but it has been too long." She shut her eyes on a sigh.

"Let me try something." Rissa held her breath. She dropped her mother's hands and raised her own to her mother's face. Rissa gently wiped both thumbs across Elizabeth's eyelids, and asked her to open her eyes again.

Elizabeth began to open them and squinted against the light. "Wait." She lifted her hand up to shield her face and peered under it. Elizabeth slowly moved her hand and looked down at Rissa. "How did you…" she trailed off and placed her hand over her mouth.

Silent tears replaced words as Elizabeth's body trembled. She shook her head back and forth, as if in denial. Words formed but never spoken behind her hand as the tears flowed. Her body convulsed as she tried to compose herself.

Rissa watched apathetically and divorced herself from the pain. Every answer she wanted plainly written on her distressed mother's body. She met her mother's eyes and took one step back before Elizabeth threw her entire body at her.

"Clary!" she wailed and wrapped Rissa tightly against her heaving frame. "Please. Forgive me! My child!" She clung tightly to Rissa and kissed her hair. Elizabeth moved back and stared into Rissa's eyes. Tears poured freely down her face and onto Rissa's clothes.

"Clary. I'm so sorry! I went back to get you." Elizabeth nodded and wiped her nose. She stopped completely. "What did they do to you? All this time?" She touched Rissa's face and pulled up her shirt sleeves.

Time. Stopped.

Elizabeth held one sleeve up while she touched the nicks and pits in Rissa's light skin. The layers fragile and damaged that even a light touch left bruises and welts. Elizabeth lightly traced a vein down to Rissa's wrist and the circular scar on it. She brought her head up and met her daughter's eyes. Tears shimmered.

"For you to be here, you escaped." Elizabeth softly touched Rissa's cheek. Her eyes hardened to light green glass. "Please tell me you killed every fucking last one of them."

Rissa smiled for the first time. "Yes, Mama."

****

Elizabeth told Rissa how she went back to save her but was met with acid. She opened her mind, and they found out Marcus died several years earlier. Saved Rissa a visit. Elizabeth pushed for details of Rissa's life, but she received few. A broad overview of a serial killer seemed good enough.

"Barb helped me escape." Rissa shook her head. "Then she revealed Mandy has power with electricity."

"Mandy what?" Elizabeth frowned and leaned forward.

"I don't know if you carry the gene, or if you and the sperm donor both carried recessive genes, but together? You created children who aren't normal." Rissa spread her hands apart. "Mandy is safe. I know someone who has helped hide her in plain sight."

"What can she do?"

"She kills it, Mama." Rissa closed her hands into fists. "She can stop an electric current with a thought." She paused. "Mandy can stop currents in buildings thirty stories high."

"She could stop a heart."

The sentence lay like wriggling maggots between them.

Rissa nodded.

Elizabeth blew out a shaky breath as more tears fled down her cheek. "You believe her to be safe?" Light green eyes implored reassurance.

"She is." Rissa would kill anyone who remotely showed interest in her sister. She would ask no questions. She would assassinate in less than a heart's beat.

Elizabeth sat back and closed her eyes. "I've made so many mistakes, and my children paid the price. I'd give anything to change your life, Clary. Anything." She looked up at her older daughter. "I don't ask for forgiveness as I can't forgive myself, but please don't tell Mandy you're sisters. I fear she will let it slip and put herself in serious danger."

"I fear the same." Rissa nodded. "I've kept my distance as best I could from them. Barb is intent on making me a part of the family." She made a face.

Elizabeth wiped her face and chuckled. "Oh, don't look so put out, child. You've slayed the dragons. Don't you deserve a bit of happiness?"

"I don't deserve anything."

"Clarissa Elizabeth Clay!"

Rissa jumped at the sound of her full name coming from her mother's mouth.

"Do you think I brought you into this world to suffer? To serve the selfish and pay for sins not your own?" Elizabeth set her jaw. "I brought my daughter into this world to live. To exist in her own space and take every inch of that space up. To know joy and revelry. To make mistakes and live through hardships."

Elizabeth stared into Rissa's soul. "You were brought into this world wrapped in love. The best parts of your father and I poured inside you. You've been through the fire and come out on the other side, scarred but alive. You being alive is enough. Existing means you deserve to have self-worth."

"Any self-worth I had disappeared with my humanity."

"I don't believe it." Elizabeth took Rissa's hand. "We are not what we have done. We are who we have become." Elizabeth stood and held Rissa's face in her hands. "You, Clarissa Elizabeth Clay, are a survivor."

CHAPTER 33

Rissa sat on the small bed and gently shook the sleeping Mandy. The girl's blonde hair spilled over her sweet face while the air whistled in and out through gently-parted lips.

Mandy wore her favorite nightgown. Rissa gave it to her a couple weeks ago on a visit, and Mandy didn't want to take it off. Ever.

It was a seasonal offering of plump orange pumpkins and sassy black cats from neck to ankle. The cats' eyes glowed green in the dark, and Mandy told everyone to leave all her lights off at night. She only used a small lamp on her nightstand, when needed.

Barb glanced at it when Rissa showed her and wiped tears away. "It's perfect."

Rissa didn't understand the tears, nor did she ask. It was the first gift she'd ever bought someone, and it made her feel a way she didn't know how to name. And Mandy's excitement and insistence on wearing all the time? Seemed perfect.

Rissa softly shook the girl once more and heard her breath change. Mandy rubbed her eyes and looked up at Rissa with a smile.

"Wissa!" The little one threw her arms around Rissa's neck and buried her face close.

Rissa wrapped her arms around Mandy and allowed herself a smile in the girl's hair. Mandy smelled of strawberry, her new favorite shampoo, and ripe oranges, her favorite body wash.

"You're making me hungry!" Rissa smacked her lips together as if starving.

Mandy pulled back and giggled. "I smell like strawberries."

"You so do." Rissa huffed the girl's hair again. "I'm going to have to find some when I get home."

"You are." Mandy nodded with all seriousness.

"Don't you want to know where your mom is?" Rissa smiled. "Barb?" She motioned around, surprised at the girl's lack of curiosity. Usually, she'd peppered Rissa with a dozen questions by now.

"She's sleeping." Mandy shrugged. "Same as I am."

Rissa froze. "What do you mean, Mandy?"

Mandy sighed. "You walk in dreams, Wissa. Right now, you're in my dream."

"How did you know that?" The words strangled and short.

Mandy leaned forward. "That's your superpower." She moved back and smiled. "I've always known that." She looked up at Rissa's ashen face. "Your hum tells me."

"My hum?" Rissa repeated through numb lips.

"Yes." Mandy nodded. "I couldn't find you for a long time, but then I heard your hum. It sounds like Mama's and mine."

"You know?" Rissa tried to gather her thoughts which lay scattered in tatters around her.

"You're my sister, Wissa." Mandy made a mad face. "They were mean to you, and I hated them."

"Them?" Rissa echoed. The pit in her stomach widened.

"The doctors and the bad guys." Mandy took Rissa's hand. "They tried to block you, but I could hear you. Then I knew you needed help."

"Help?"

"I sent Mama to you." The little girl dropped Rissa's hand and clapped hers in delight. "And you knew exactly what to do."

"You sent Barb?" Pieces of the puzzle fell into place slowly.

"I had to..." Mandy averted her eyes for a second before she looked back at Rissa, "do something to help her find that job."

"What did you do, Mandy?" Rissa's mind raced.

"Nothing bad." Mandy bit her lip. "One of the nurses reads the newspaper every day. The rest read it on their phone, but Lucy reads the real paper." She sighed. "They wanted nurses for you, and I saw the ad. When Mama came, I asked for us to go see Lucy."

Mandy glanced up. "I told Mama that Lucy asked to see her about flowers. Mama loves flowers."

"And then?" Rissa asked thinly.

"I waited until Mama saw Lucy reading the paper, and I made Lucy's head fall."

"Made her head fall?" Rissa repeated.

Mandy nodded briskly. "Then Mama called the doctors to help her, and I took the newspaper. When they took Lucy away, I showed Mama the newspaper. She told me I was a smart girl."

Smart girl? Rissa fought to remain calm. "What did you do to Lucy, Mandy?"

"I pushed." Mandy sighed. "But I think I pushed too hard." She smoothed her nightgown over her legs. "I made her too quiet," Mandy motioned to her head, "in here."

The image of Mandy killing the alarm clock resonated in Rissa's head. Everything vibrated. Pulsed. Even people. Especially people. A bunch of moving atoms and subatomic particles. Until someone stopped them.

"I'm sure she'll be fine." Rissa pulled the young girl close and held her tight. She wouldn't let her legacy continue with Mandy.

Never let the little one know the darker side of existence.

"I pushed people before." Mandy pulled back and studied Rissa with cool bottle-green eyes. "I had to practice."

Rissa's heart stopped and then raced. "Practice? Have you pushed a lot of people?"

"Yeah." Mandy sighed. "Some you have to push super hard. Some soft. I never know which is which."

A superpower in the hands of an eleven-year-old. Eager to help but unsure of her strength. Mandy pushed people, as sure as Rissa pushed Dr. Hamilton. Bile rose in Rissa's throat.

"How many have you pushed, Mandy?"

"Oh." The little girl's hand fluttered in the air. "Lots." She nodded. "Mean people, mostly. They smile to your face, but their eyes are wrong. I pushed the hardest when you escaped. Pushed so hard I had a bloody nose."

All color drained from Rissa as if siphoned in an instant. "You... helped?"

"The bad hum. I stopped it." Mandy patted Rissa's leg.

At a loss for words, Rissa could only force a smile and thank her younger sister.

Mandy leaned forward and hugged her tight. "You're my sister, Wissa. I would do anything for you."

The words, instead of reassuring, scared the hell out of Rissa.

"We're a team." The little girl snuggled closer. "More bad men are coming. I already pushed some."

Rissa jerked back in shock. "What?

"They're coming for you, Wissa." Dark green eyes blackened briefly as Mandy spoke. "They don't know your hum, but they're looking everywhere." She paused. "Not the same bad men. Different." Mandy tilted her head to the side. "You hurt them."

The list long and never-ending, Rissa took a breath and asked the question she feared. "Who did I hurt?" *Who didn't I hurt?*

"The girls. You hurt their girls."

****

8/25/25

Crystal Inman*

www.ingramcontent.com/pod-product-compliance
Lightning Source LLC
Chambersburg PA
CBHW022146240626
47153CB00007B/2540